UP AND AT 'EM Marmaduke

by

BRAD ANDERSON

TOR ®

A TOM DOHERTY ASSOCIATES BOOK
NEW YORK

This is a work of fiction. All the characters and events portrayed in this book are fictional, and any resemblance to real people or incidents is purely coincidental.

MARMADUKE: UP AND AT 'EM

Copyright © 1986 by United Feature Syndicate, Inc.

All rights reserved, including the right to reproduce this book or portions thereof in any form.

A TOR Book
Published by Tom Doherty Associates, Inc.
49 West 24 Street
New York, NY 10010

Cover art by Brad Anderson

ISBN: 0-812-50597-2   Can. ISBN: 0-812-50598-0

First edition: February 1990

Printed in the United States of America

0 9 8 7 6 5 4 3 2 1

Look for all these Marmaduke books from Tor

Marmaduke Hams It Up!
Marmaduke Laps It Up!
Marmaduke: I Am Lovable
Marmaduke: It's a Dog's Life
Sitting Pretty, Marmaduke

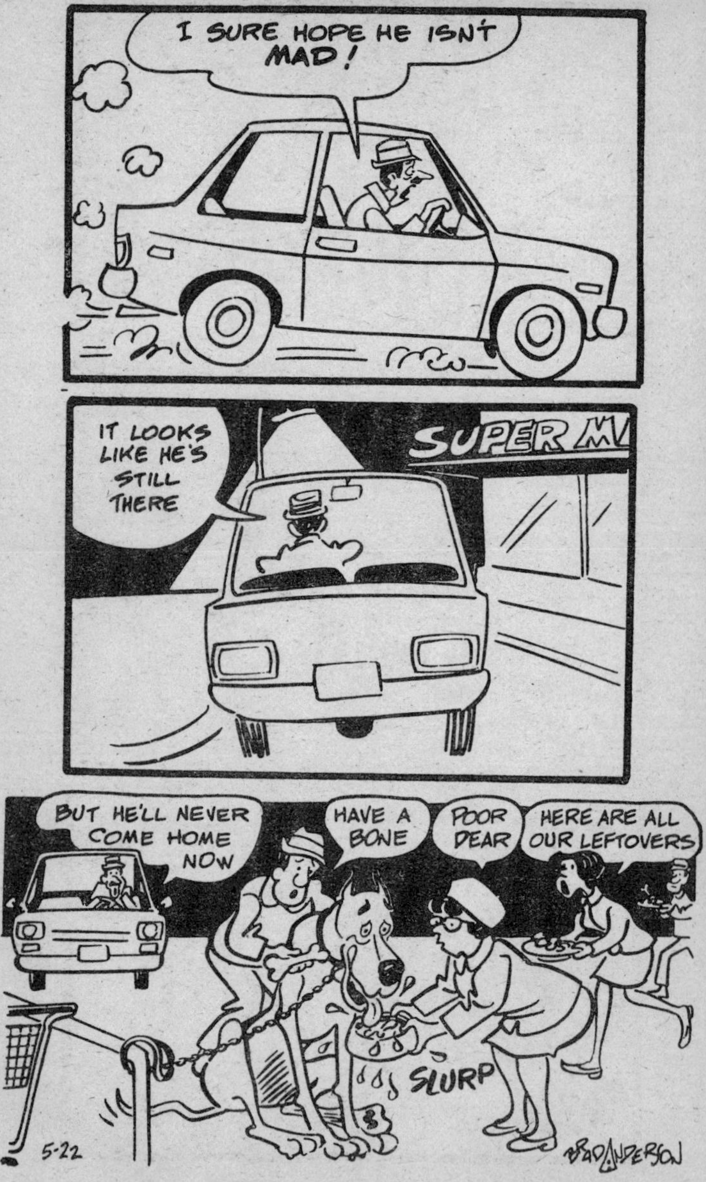
I SURE HOPE HE ISN'T MAD!
IT LOOKS LIKE HE'S STILL THERE
SUPER M
BUT HE'LL NEVER COME HOME NOW
HAVE A BONE
POOR DEAR
HERE ARE ALL OUR LEFTOVERS
SLURP
5-22
BRAD ANDERSON

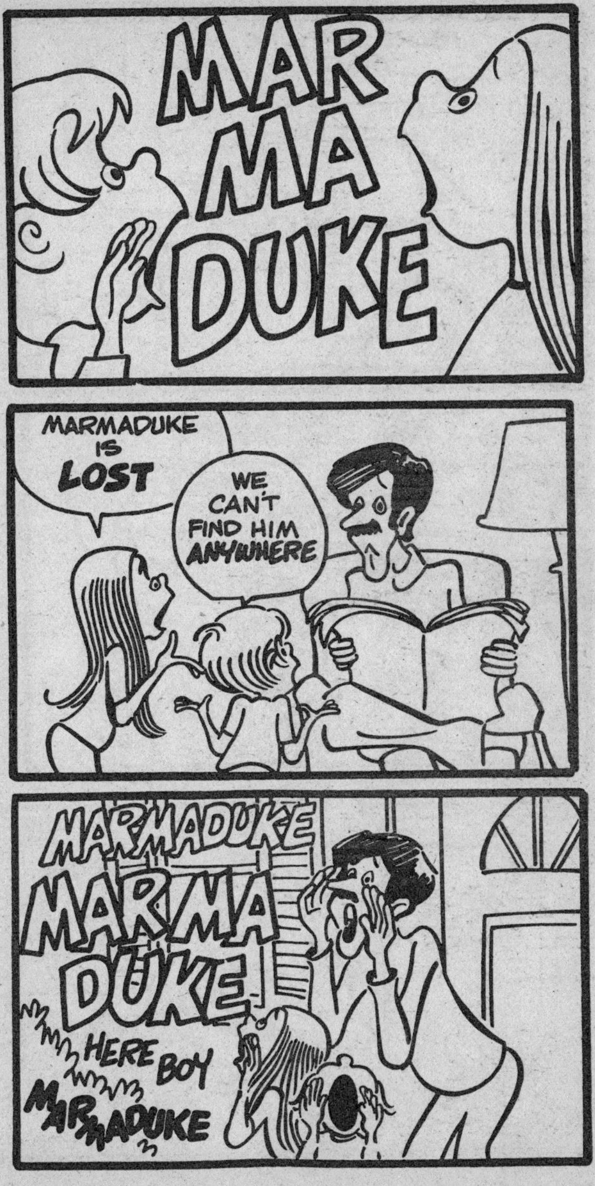
MAR
MA
DUKE
MARMADUKE IS LOST
WE CAN'T FIND HIM ANYWHERE
MARMADUKE
MARMA
DUKE
HERE BOY
MARMADUKE

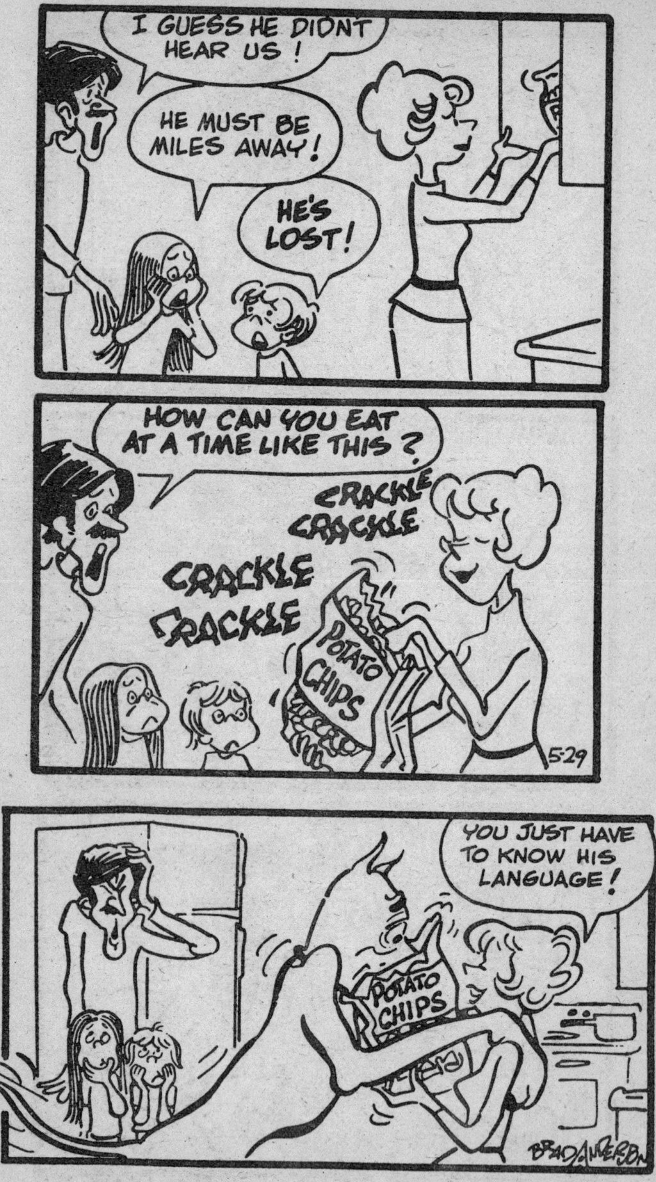
I GUESS HE DIDN'T HEAR US !
HE MUST BE MILES AWAY !
HE'S LOST !
HOW CAN YOU EAT AT A TIME LIKE THIS ?
CRACKLE CRACKLE
CRACKLE CRACKLE
POTATO CHIPS
5-29
YOU JUST HAVE TO KNOW HIS LANGUAGE !
POTATO CHIPS
BRAD ANDERSON

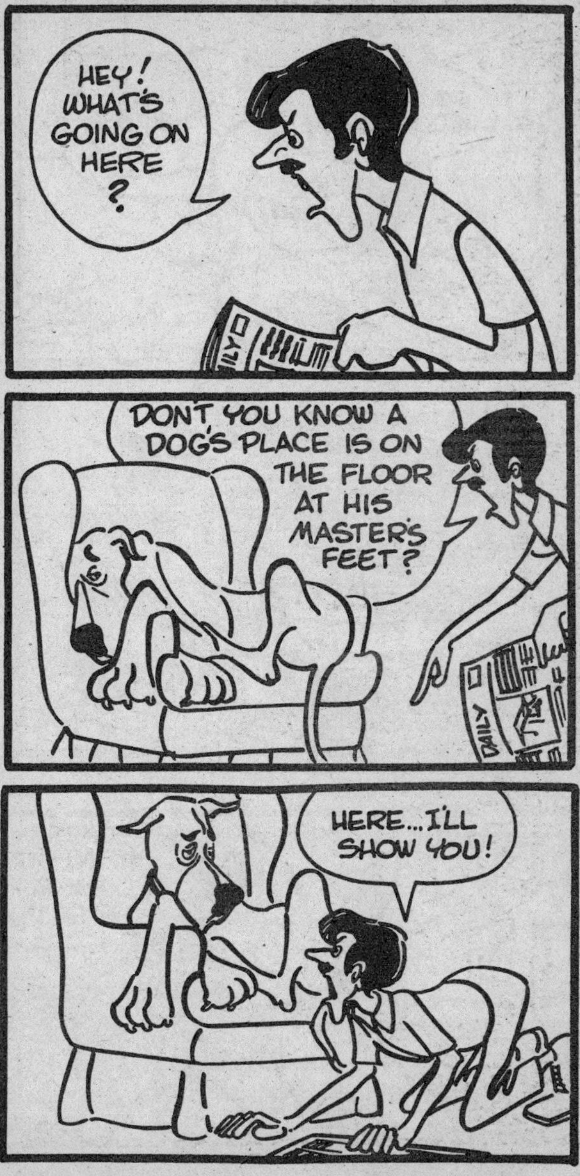
HEY! WHAT'S GOING ON HERE ?
DAILY
DON'T YOU KNOW A DOG'S PLACE IS ON THE FLOOR AT HIS MASTER'S FEET?
DAILY
HERE...I'LL SHOW YOU!

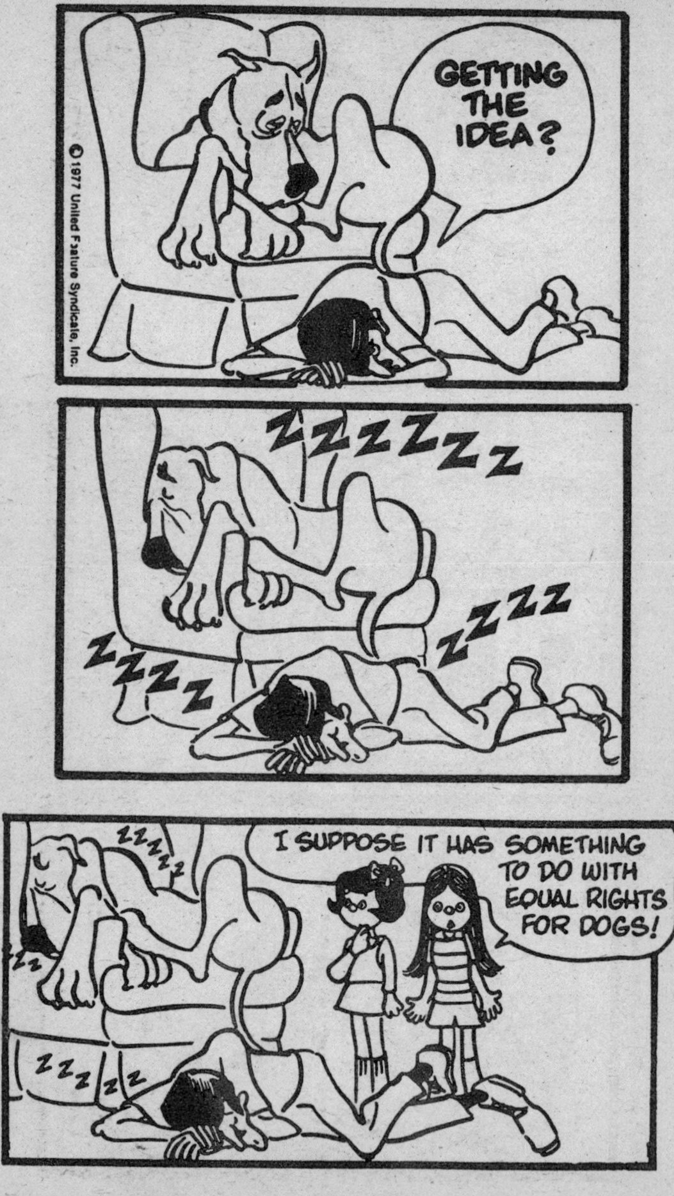
GETTING THE IDEA?
ZZZZZZz
ZZZZZ
ZZZZZ
ZZZZZz
Zz
ZZZzz
I SUPPOSE IT HAS SOMETHING TO DO WITH EQUAL RIGHTS FOR DOGS!

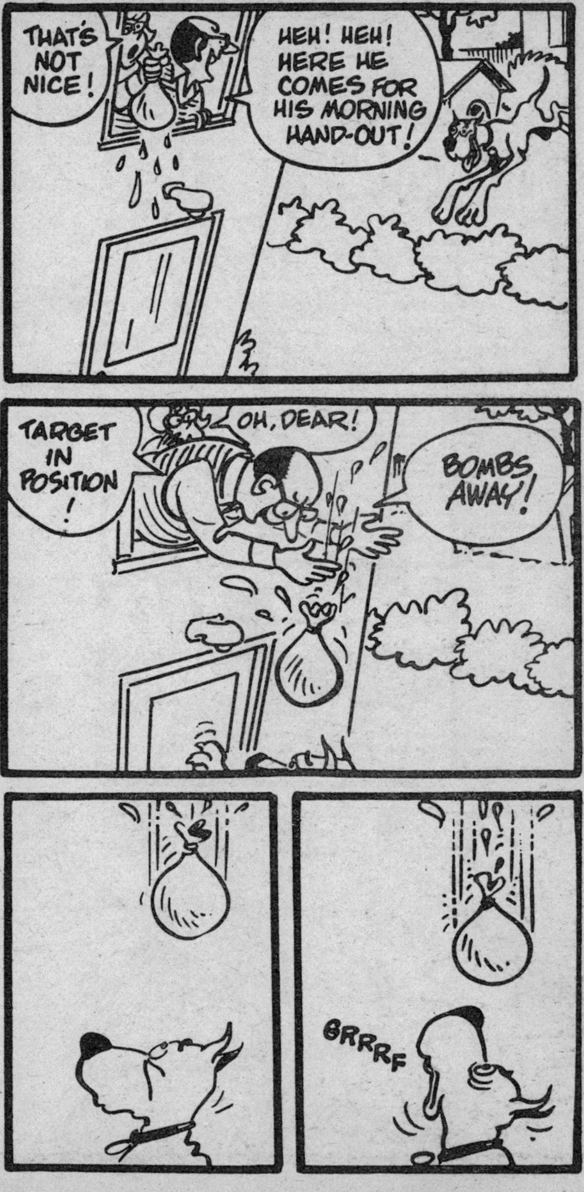
THAT'S NOT NICE!
HEH! HEH! HERE HE COMES FOR HIS MORNING HAND-OUT!
TARGET IN POSITION!
OH, DEAR!
BOMBS AWAY!
GRRRRF

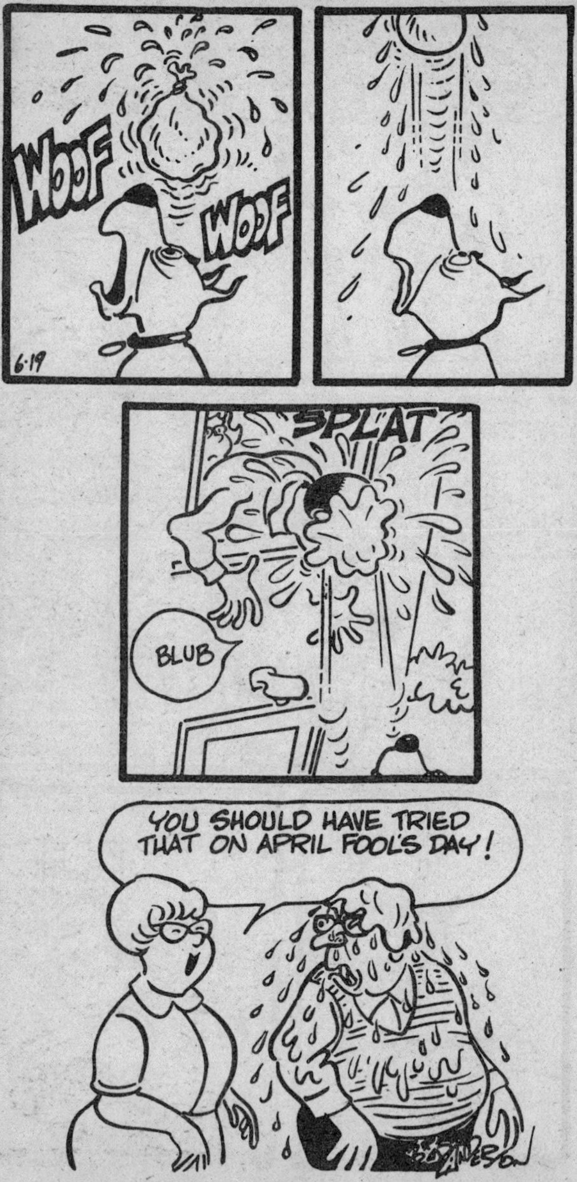
WOOF
WOOF
6·19
SPLAT
BLUB
YOU SHOULD HAVE TRIED THAT ON APRIL FOOL'S DAY!
BOB ANDERSON

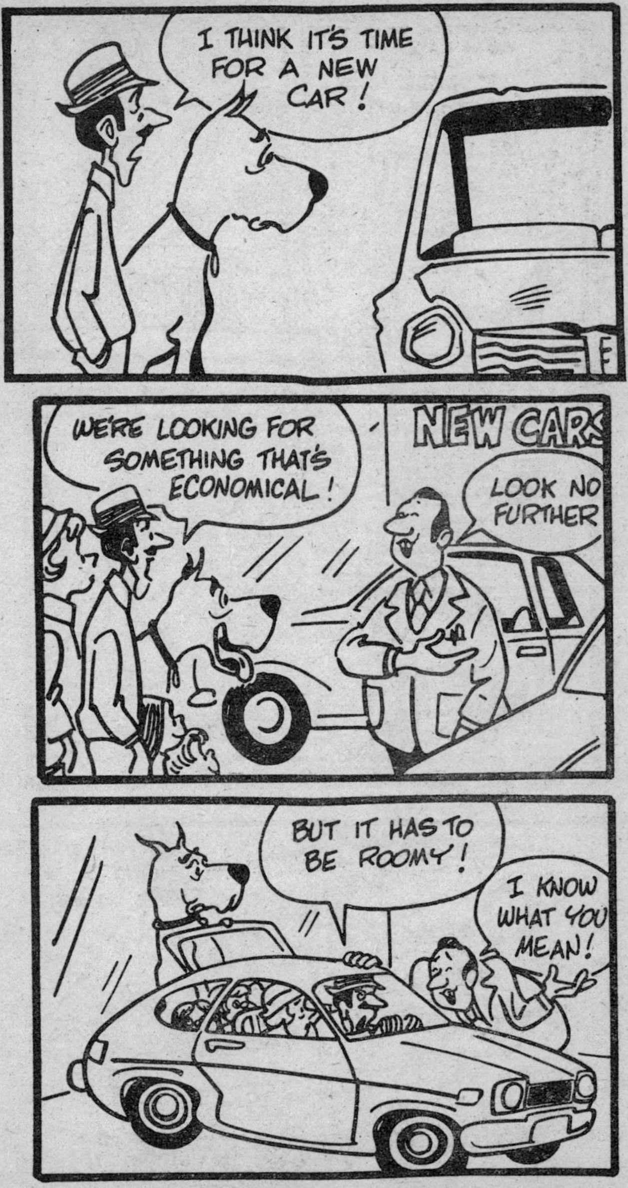
I THINK IT'S TIME FOR A NEW CAR!
WE'RE LOOKING FOR SOMETHING THAT'S ECONOMICAL!
NEW CARS
LOOK NO FURTHER
BUT IT HAS TO BE ROOMY!
I KNOW WHAT YOU MEAN!

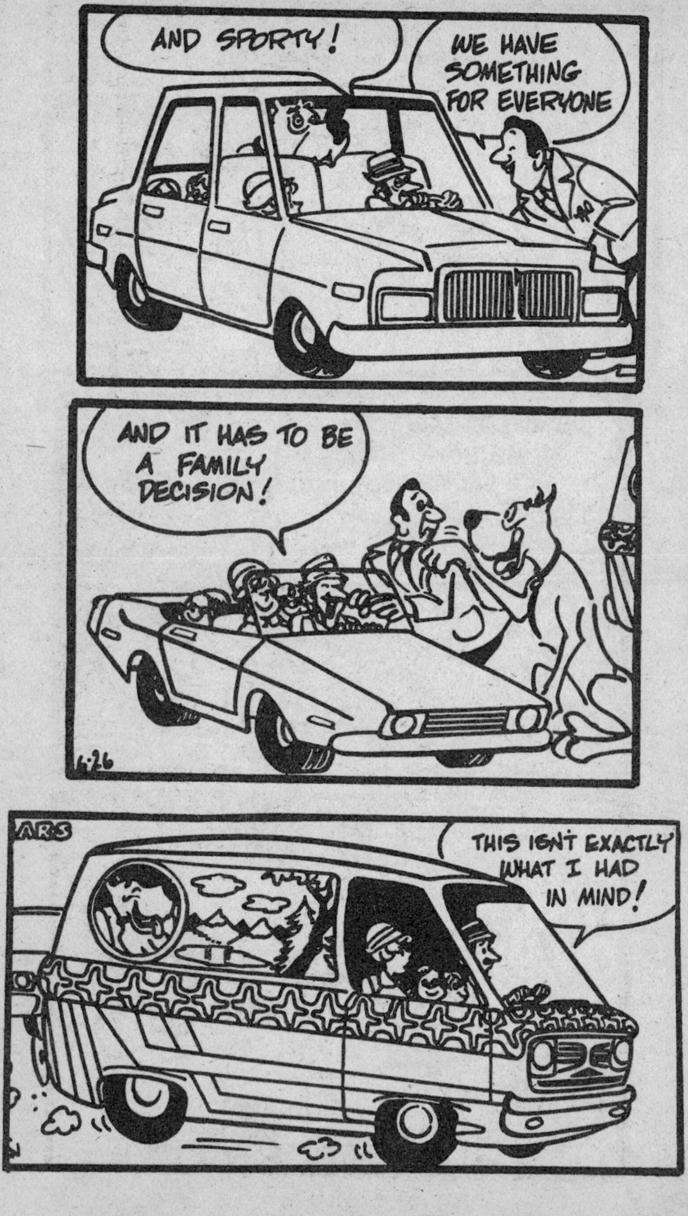
AND SPORTY!
WE HAVE SOMETHING FOR EVERYONE
AND IT HAS TO BE A FAMILY DECISION!
THIS ISN'T EXACTLY WHAT I HAD IN MIND!

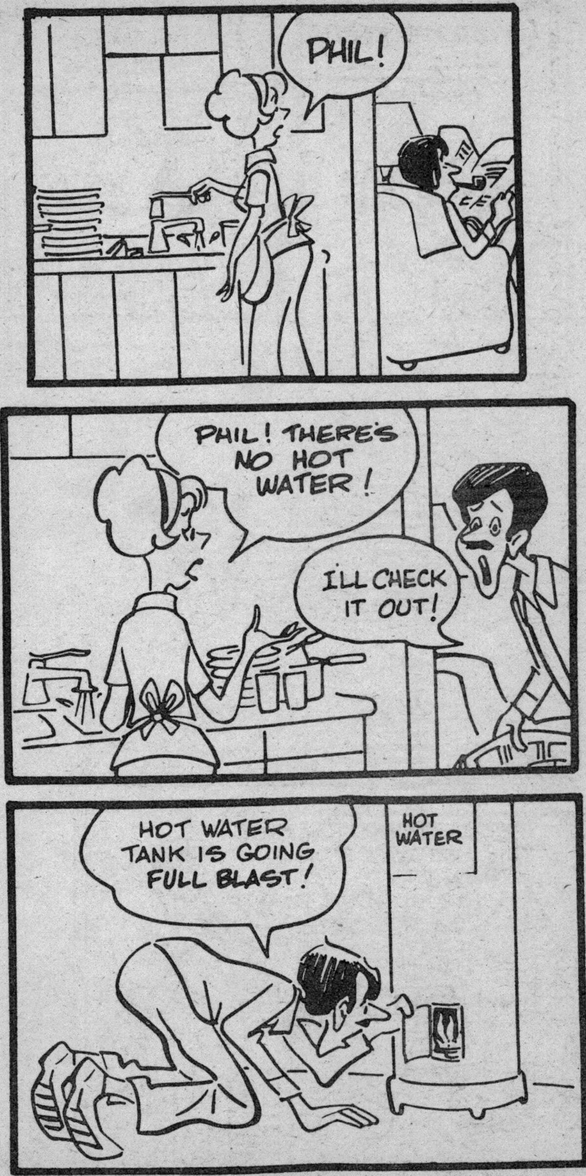
PHIL!
PHIL! THERE'S NO HOT WATER!
I'LL CHECK IT OUT!
HOT WATER TANK IS GOING FULL BLAST!
HOT WATER

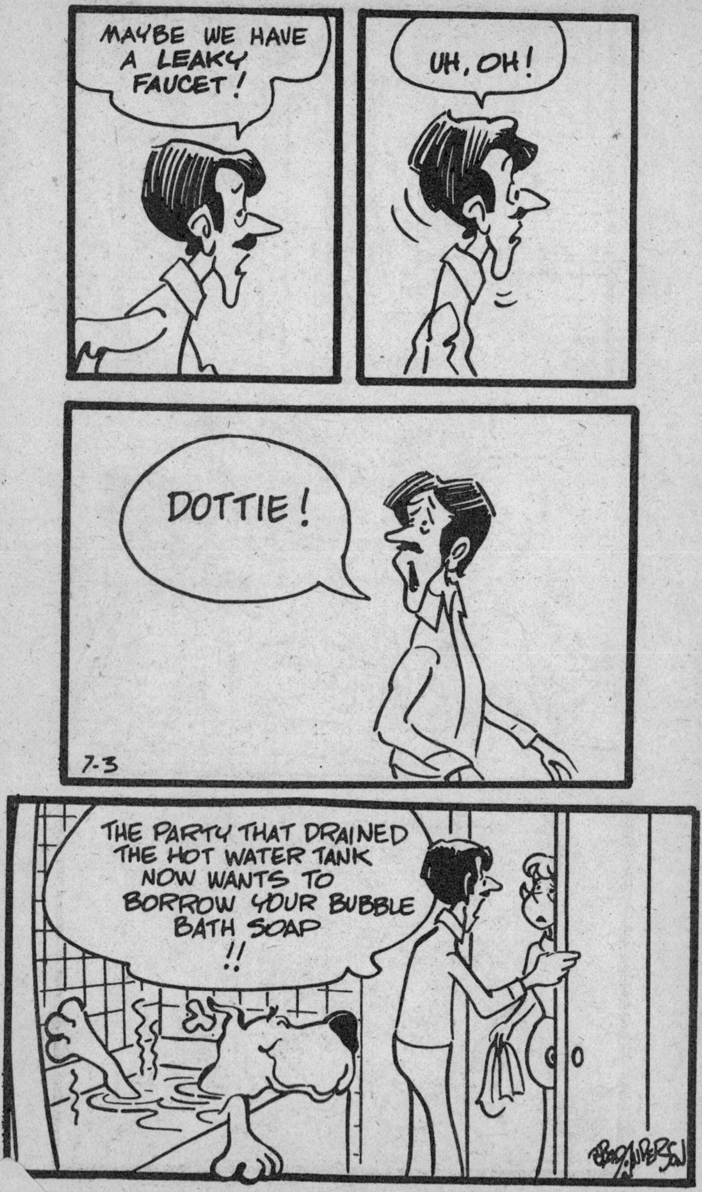
MAYBE WE HAVE A LEAKY FAUCET!
UH, OH!
DOTTIE!
7-3
THE PARTY THAT DRAINED THE HOT WATER TANK NOW WANTS TO BORROW YOUR BUBBLE BATH SOAP !!

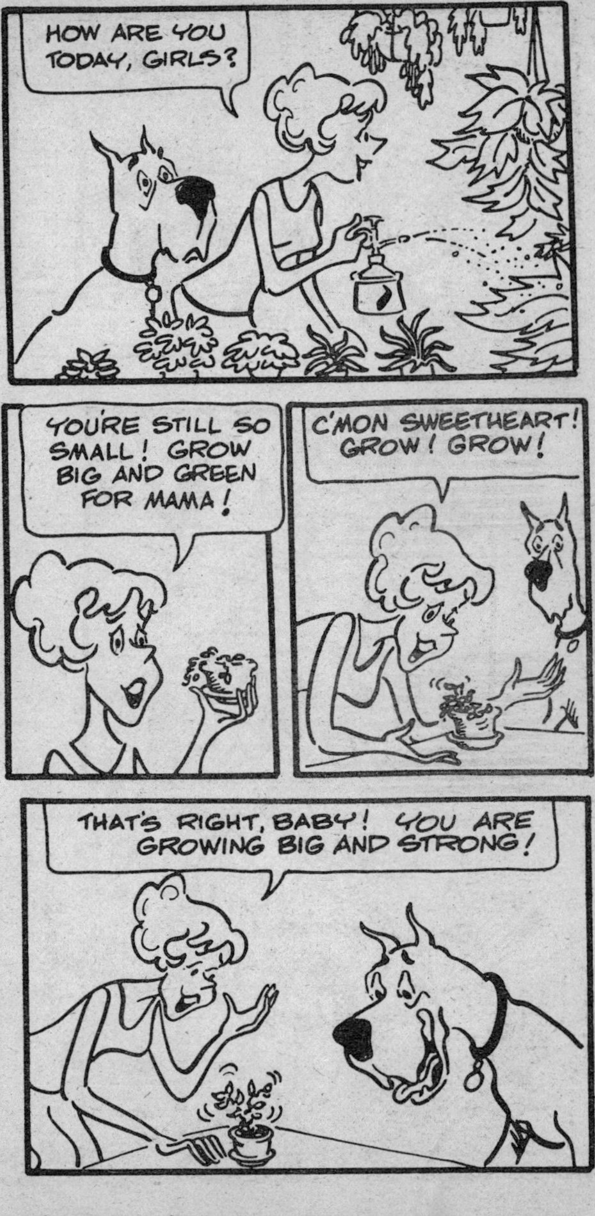
HOW ARE YOU TODAY, GIRLS?
YOU'RE STILL SO SMALL! GROW BIG AND GREEN FOR MAMA!
C'MON SWEETHEART! GROW! GROW!
THAT'S RIGHT, BABY! YOU ARE GROWING BIG AND STRONG!

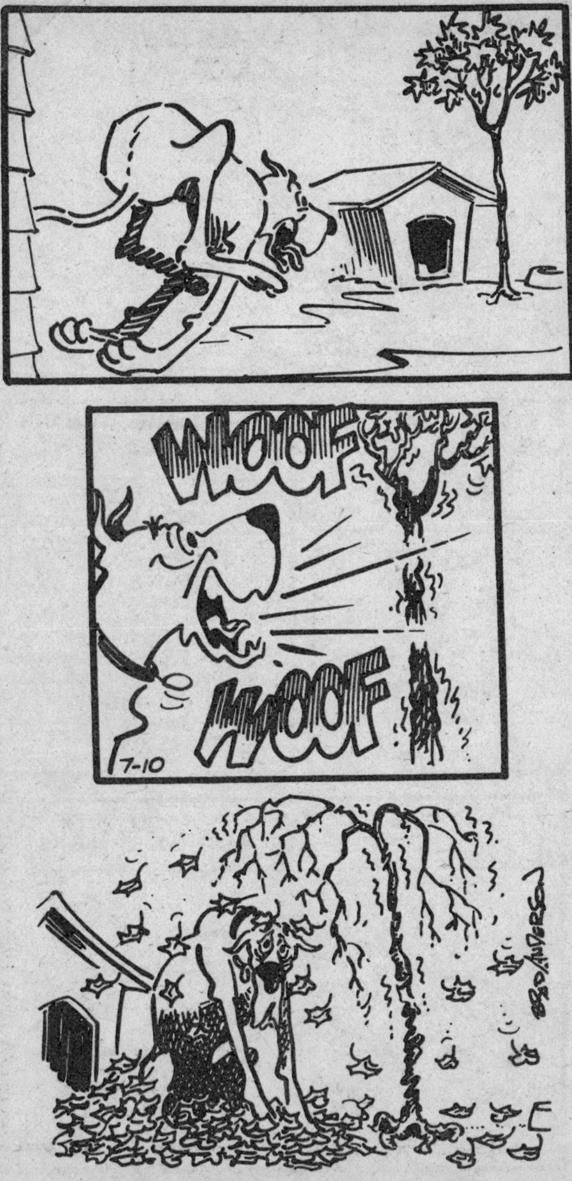
WOOF
WOOF
7-10

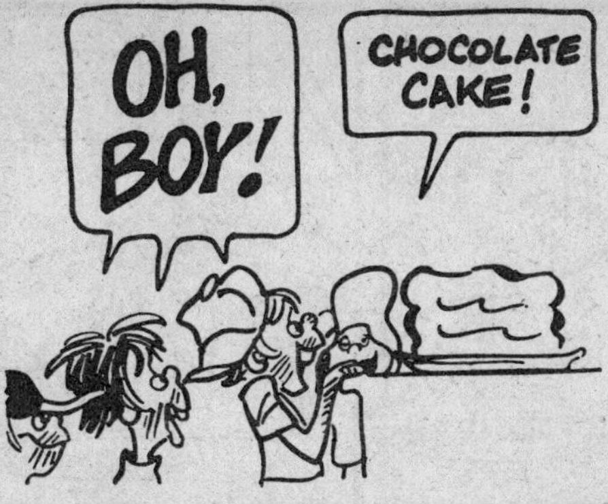
OH, BOY!
CHOCOLATE CAKE!

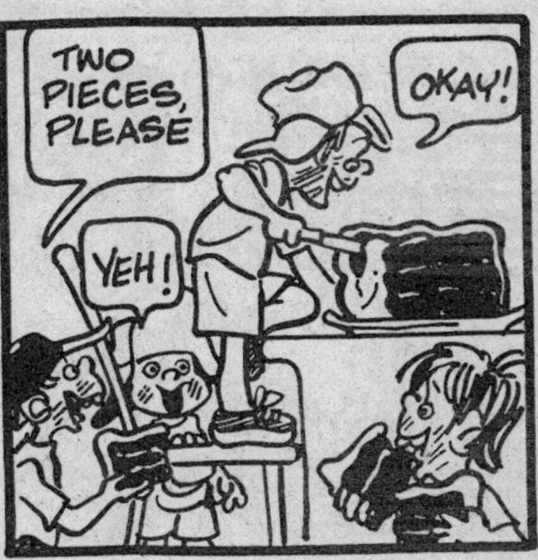
TWO PIECES, PLEASE
OKAY!
YEH!

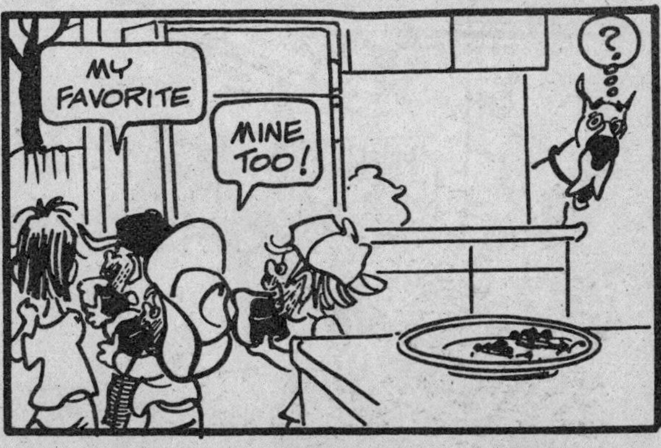
MY FAVORITE
MINE TOO!
?

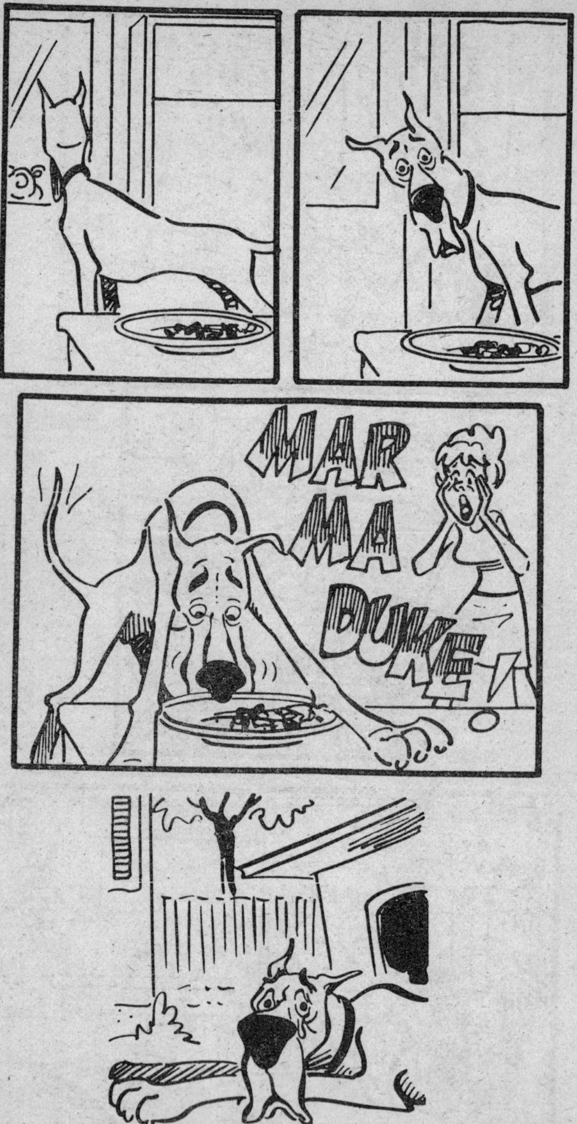
MARMADUKE!
7-24
BRAD ANDERSON

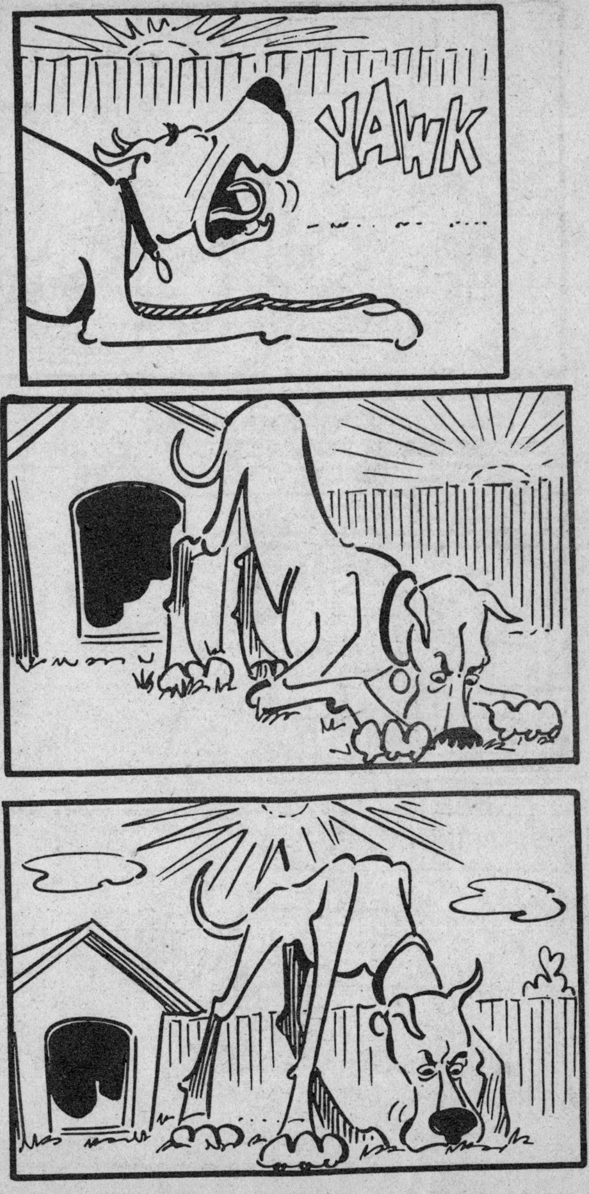
YAWK

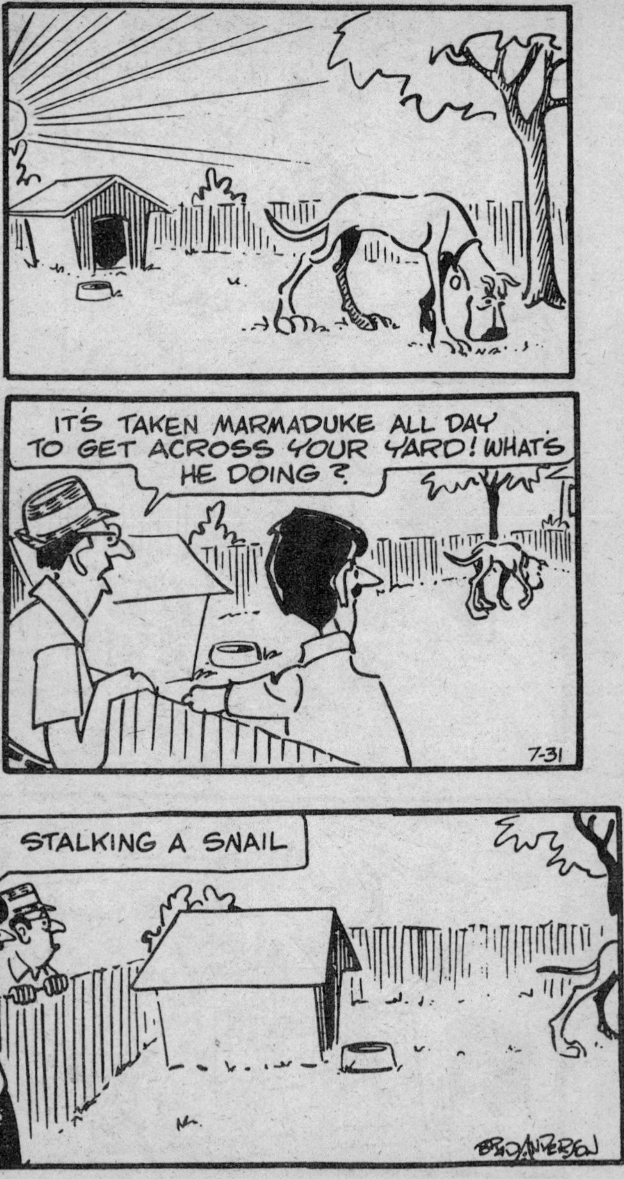
IT'S TAKEN MARMADUKE ALL DAY TO GET ACROSS YOUR YARD! WHAT'S HE DOING?
7-31
STALKING A SNAIL
BRAD ANDERSON

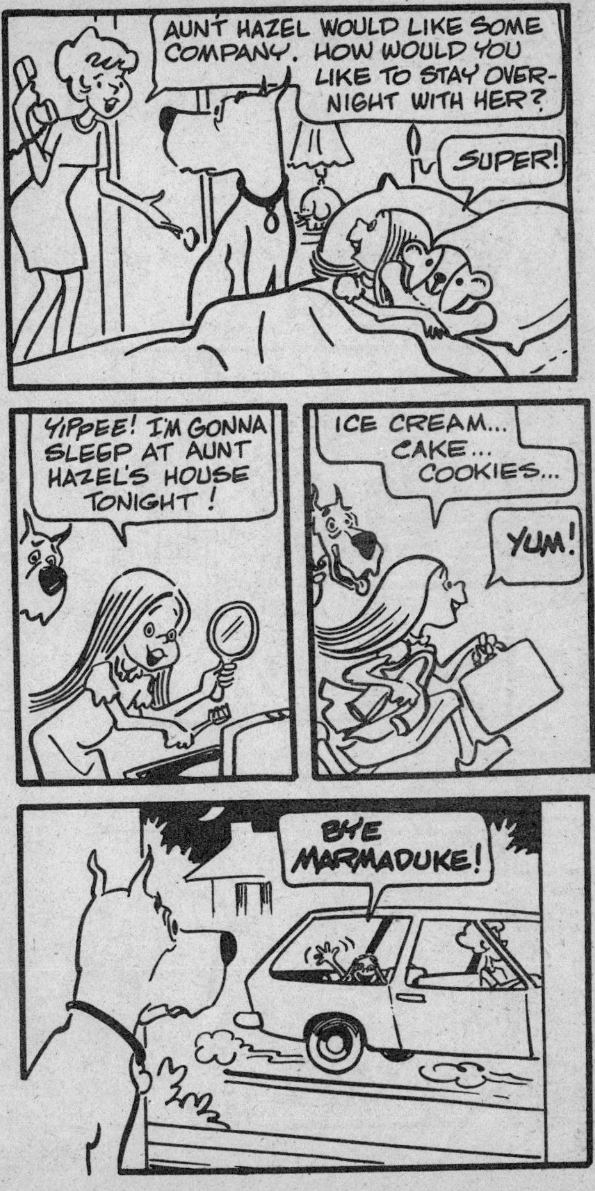
AUNT HAZEL WOULD LIKE SOME COMPANY. HOW WOULD YOU LIKE TO STAY OVER-NIGHT WITH HER?
SUPER!
YIPPEE! I'M GONNA SLEEP AT AUNT HAZEL'S HOUSE TONIGHT!
ICE CREAM... CAKE... COOKIES...
YUM!
BYE MARMADUKE!

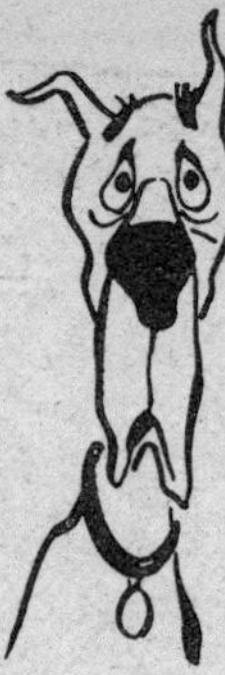

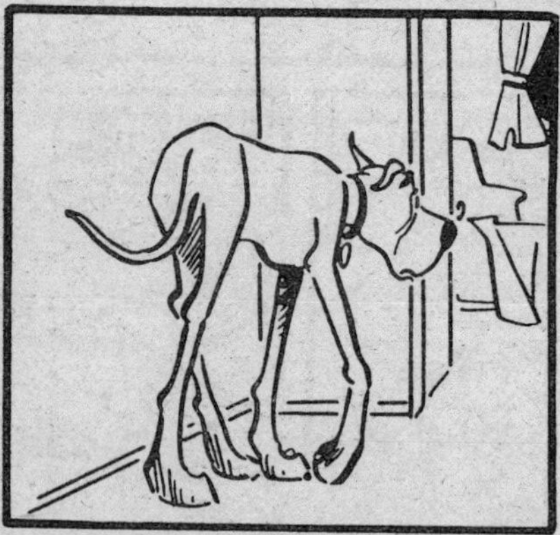

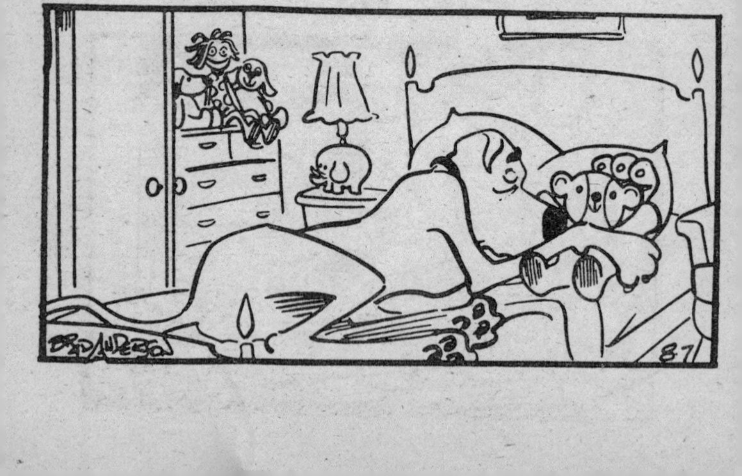
BRAD ANDERSON

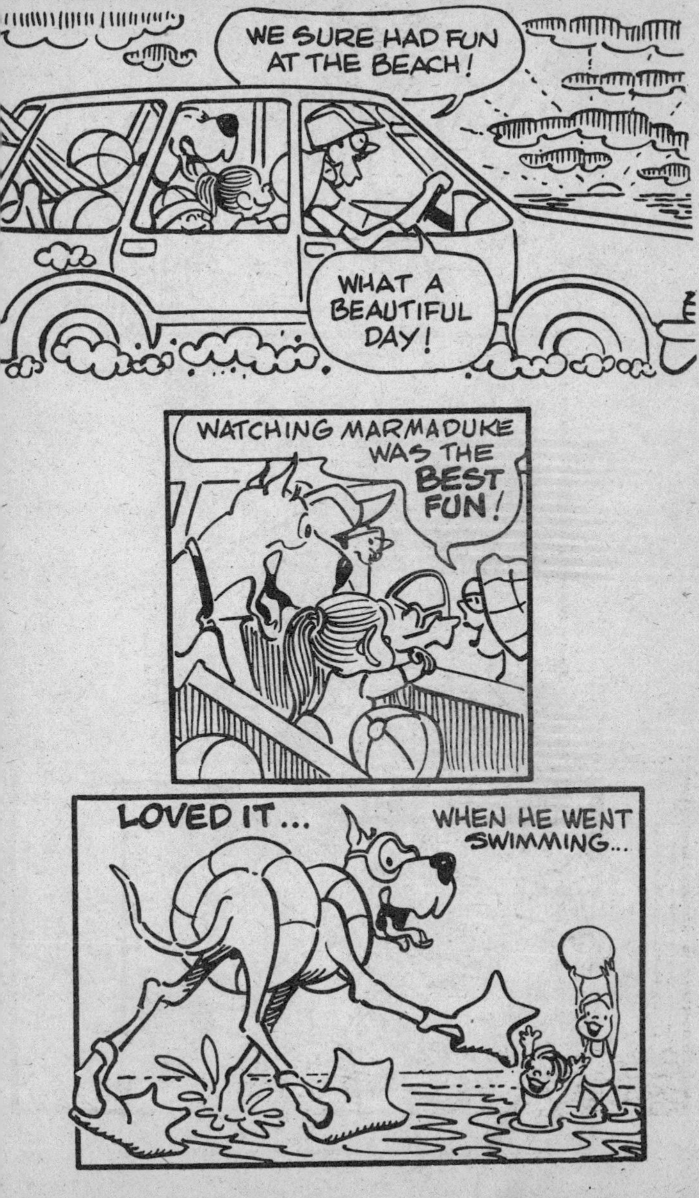
WE SURE HAD FUN AT THE BEACH!
WHAT A BEAUTIFUL DAY!
WATCHING MARMADUKE WAS THE BEST FUN!
LOVED IT...
WHEN HE WENT SWIMMING...

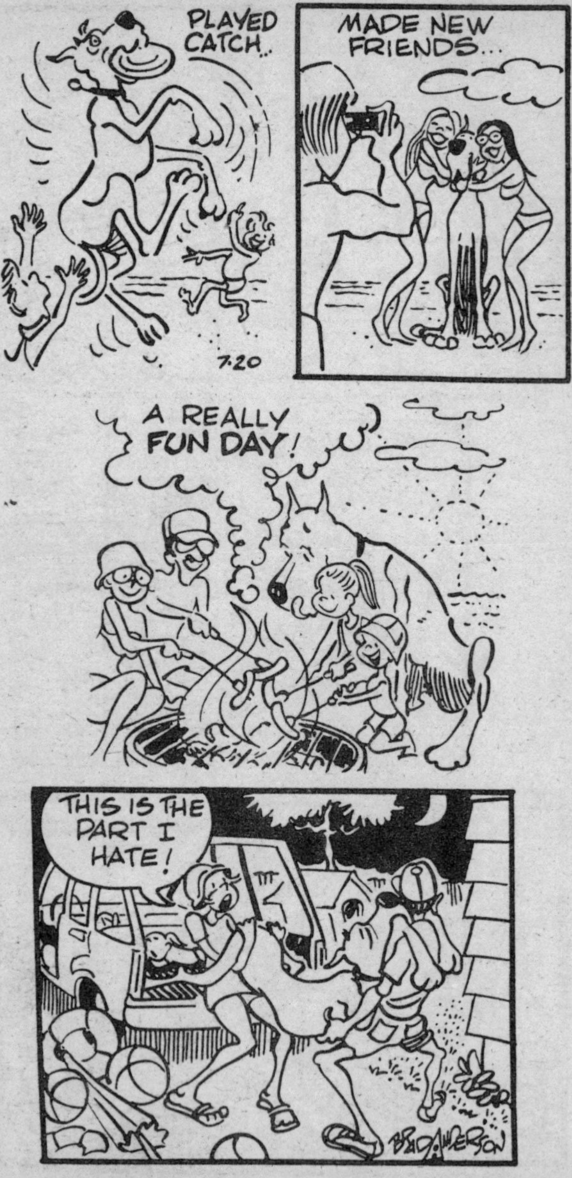
PLAYED CATCH...
7·20
MADE NEW FRIENDS...
A REALLY FUN DAY!
THIS IS THE PART I HATE!
BRAD ANDERSON

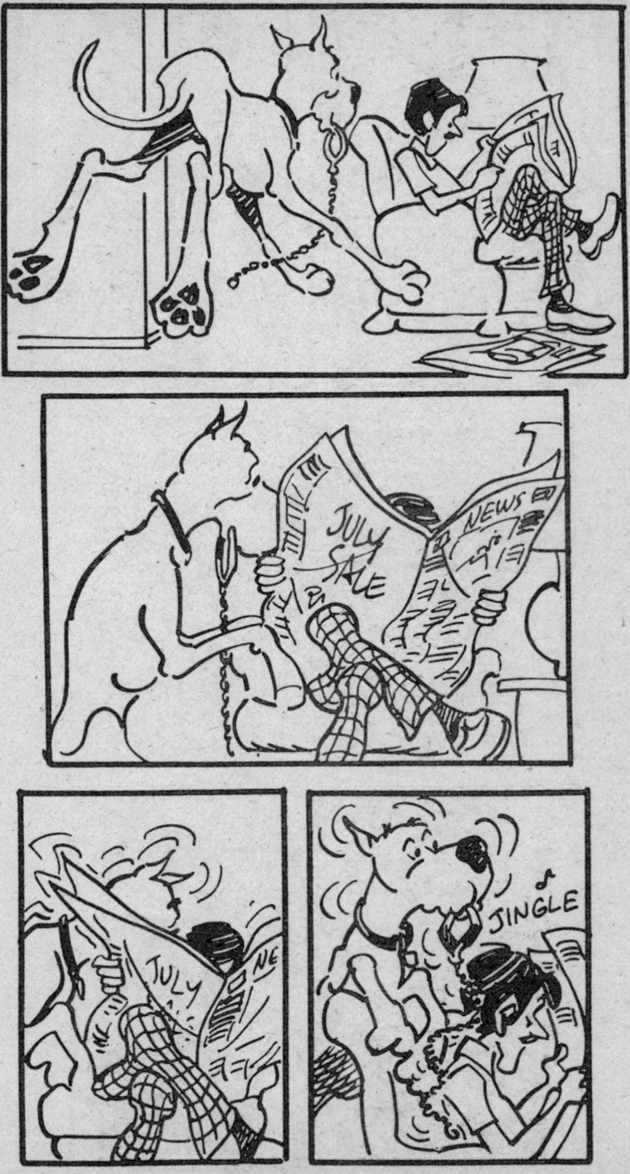
JULY SALE
NEWS
JULY
NE
JINGLE

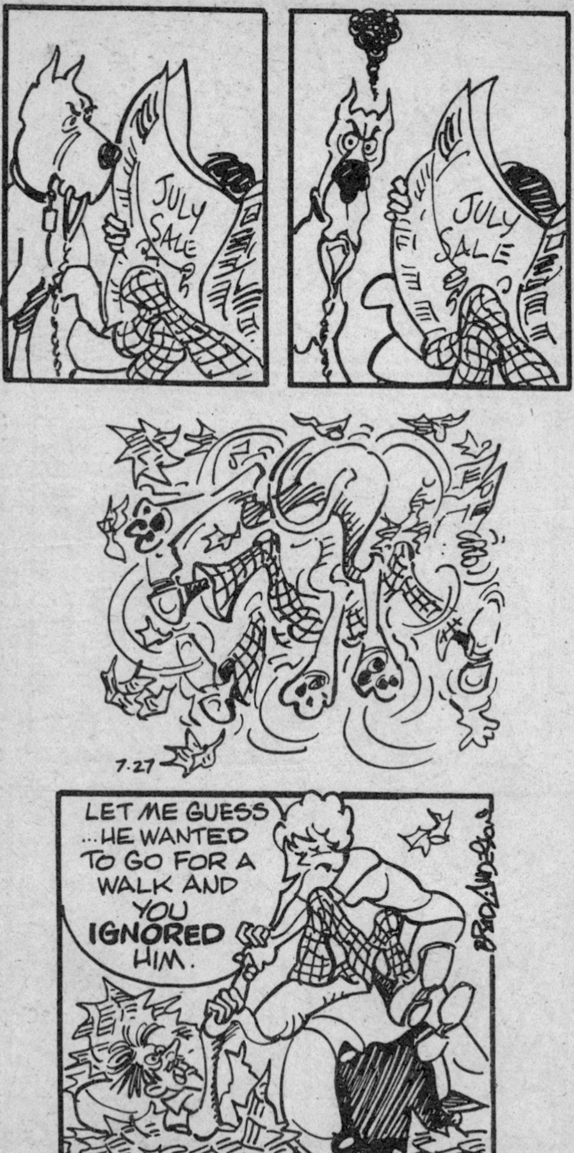
JULY SALE
JULY SALE
7·27
LET ME GUESS ...HE WANTED TO GO FOR A WALK AND YOU **IGNORED** HIM.

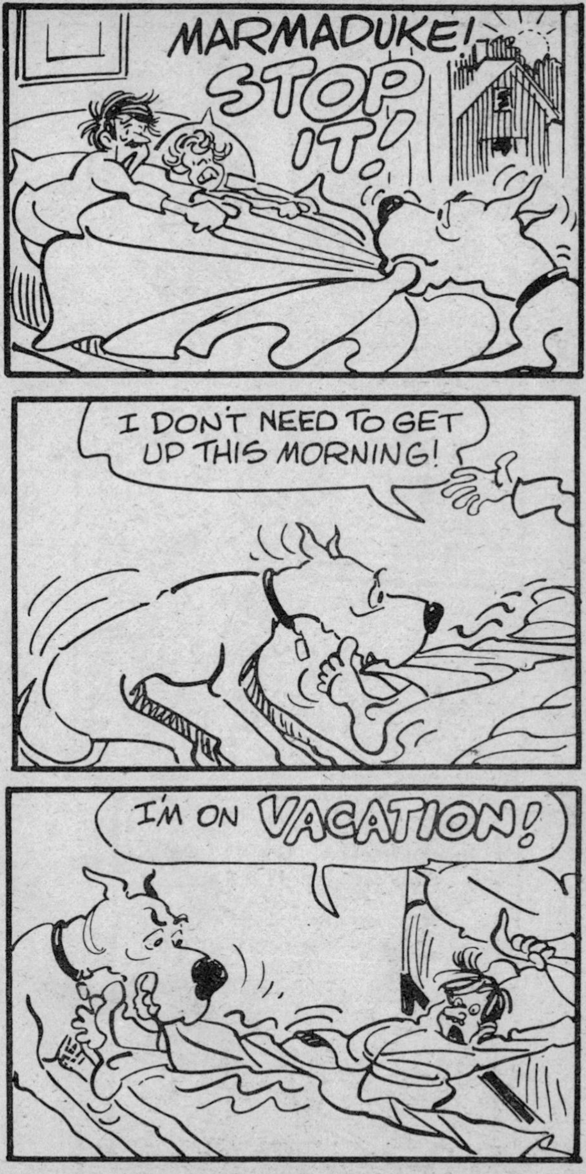
MARMADUKE! STOP IT!
I DON'T NEED TO GET UP THIS MORNING!
I'M ON VACATION!

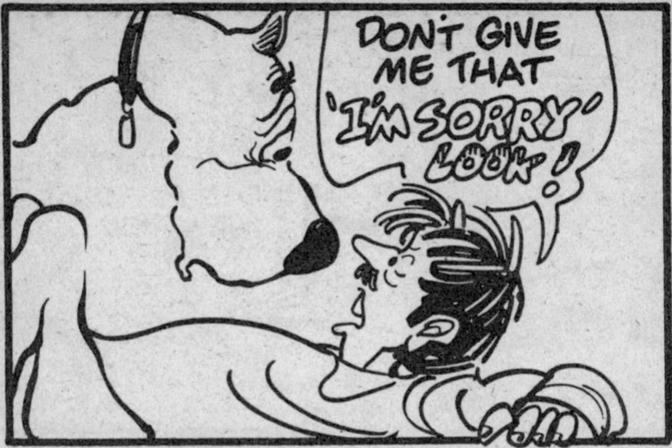
DON'T GIVE ME THAT 'I'M SORRY' LOOK!

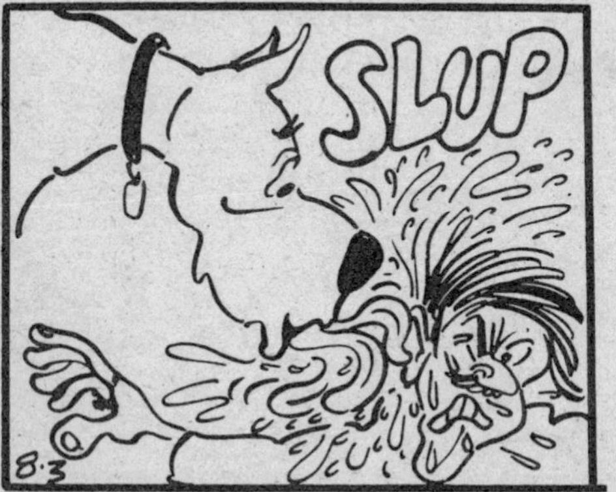
SLUP
8·3

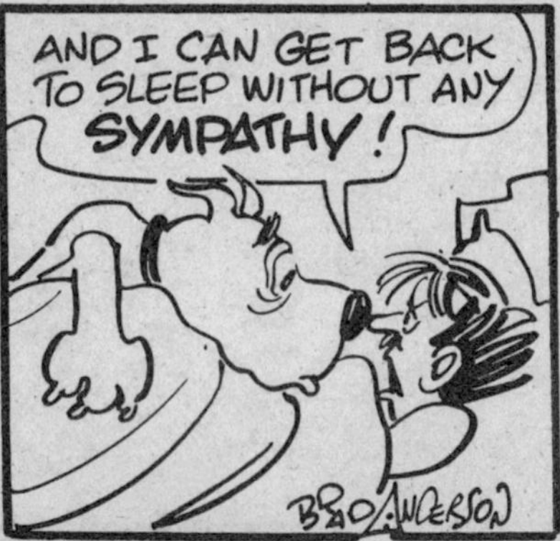
AND I CAN GET BACK TO SLEEP WITHOUT ANY SYMPATHY!
BRAD ANDERSON

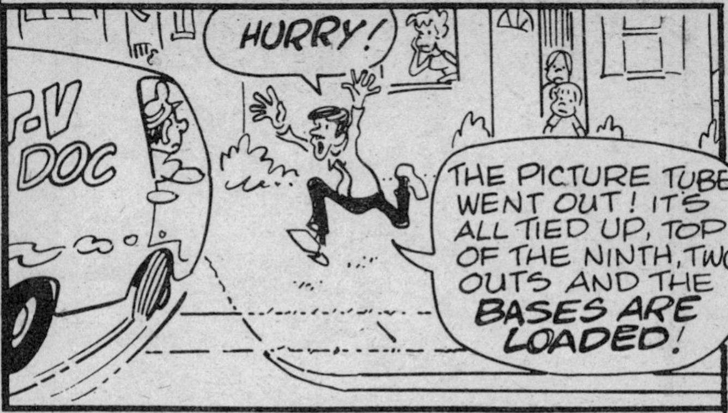
DOC
HURRY!
THE PICTURE TUBE WENT OUT! IT'S ALL TIED UP, TOP OF THE NINTH, TWO OUTS AND THE BASES ARE LOADED!

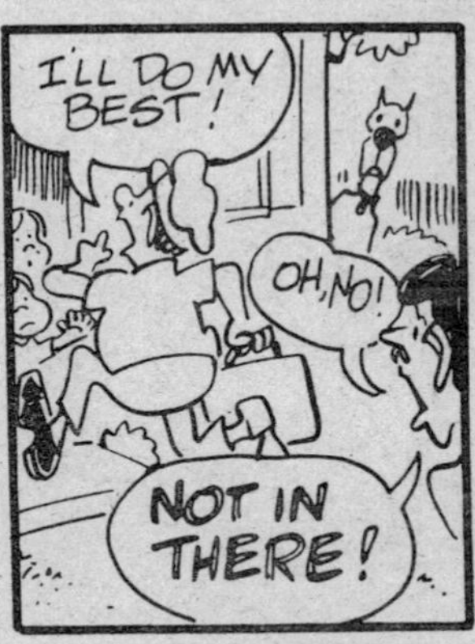
I'LL DO MY BEST!
OH, NO!
NOT IN THERE!

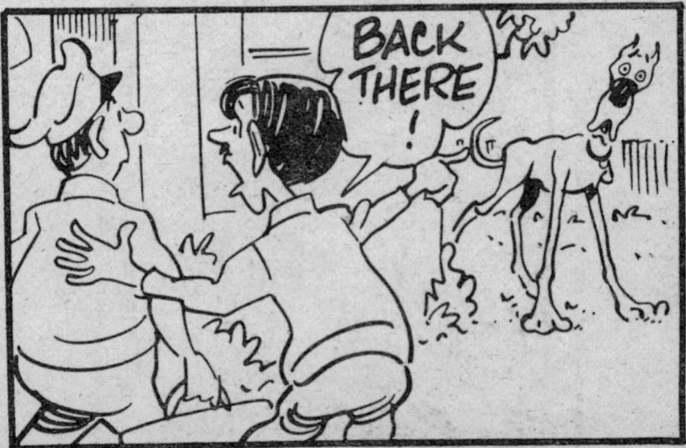
BACK THERE!

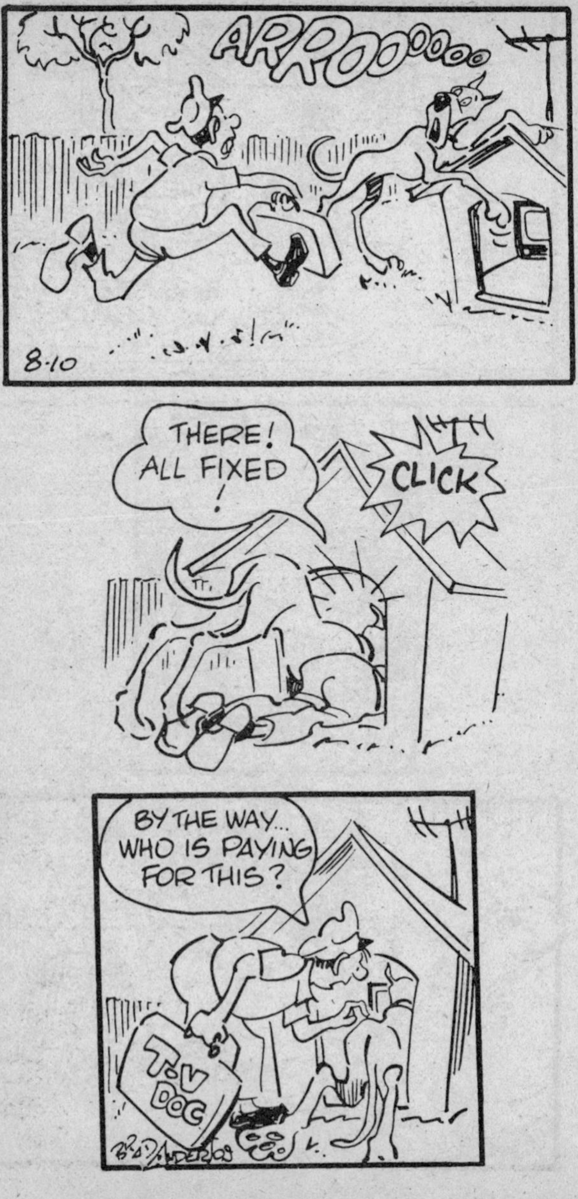
ARROOoooo
8·10
THERE! ALL FIXED!
CLICK
BY THE WAY... WHO IS PAYING FOR THIS?
T.V DOC

HEY! MOM SAID I'M THE BOSS!
GET OFF THE COUCH!
RUFFFFF
OH, NO! MOM IS GONNA BE HOME ANY MINUTE!

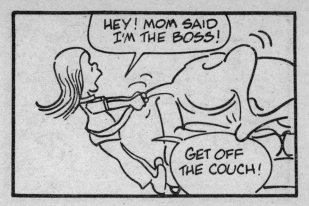

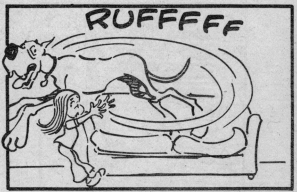

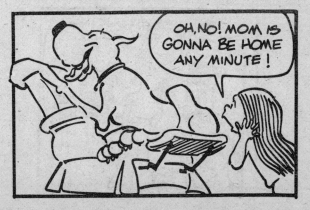

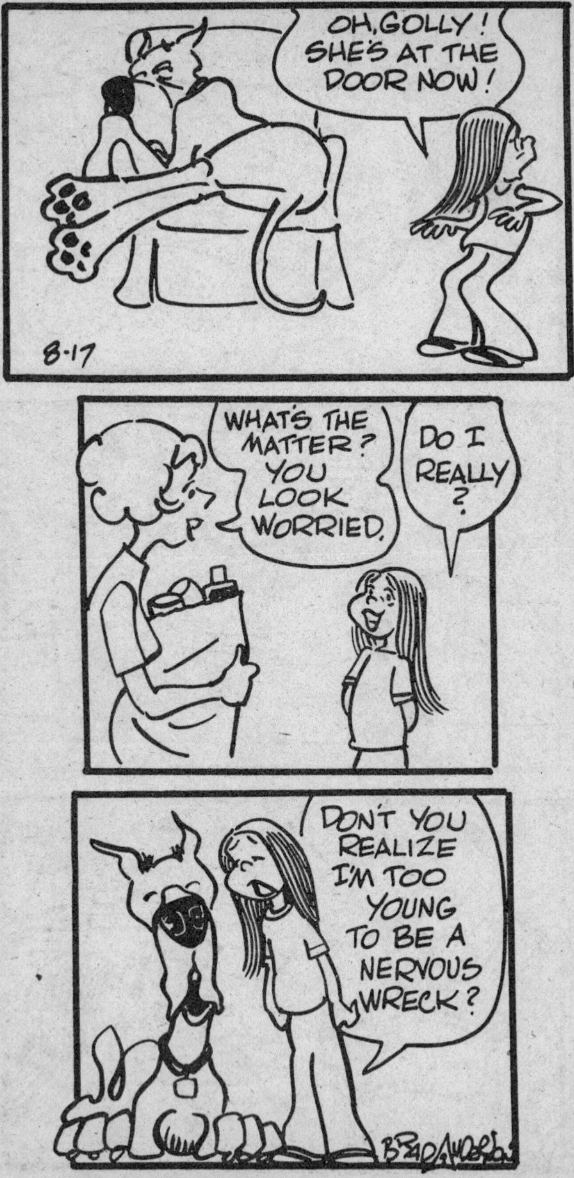
OH, GOLLY! SHE'S AT THE DOOR NOW!
8-17
WHAT'S THE MATTER? YOU LOOK WORRIED.
DO I REALLY?
DON'T YOU REALIZE I'M TOO YOUNG TO BE A NERVOUS WRECK?

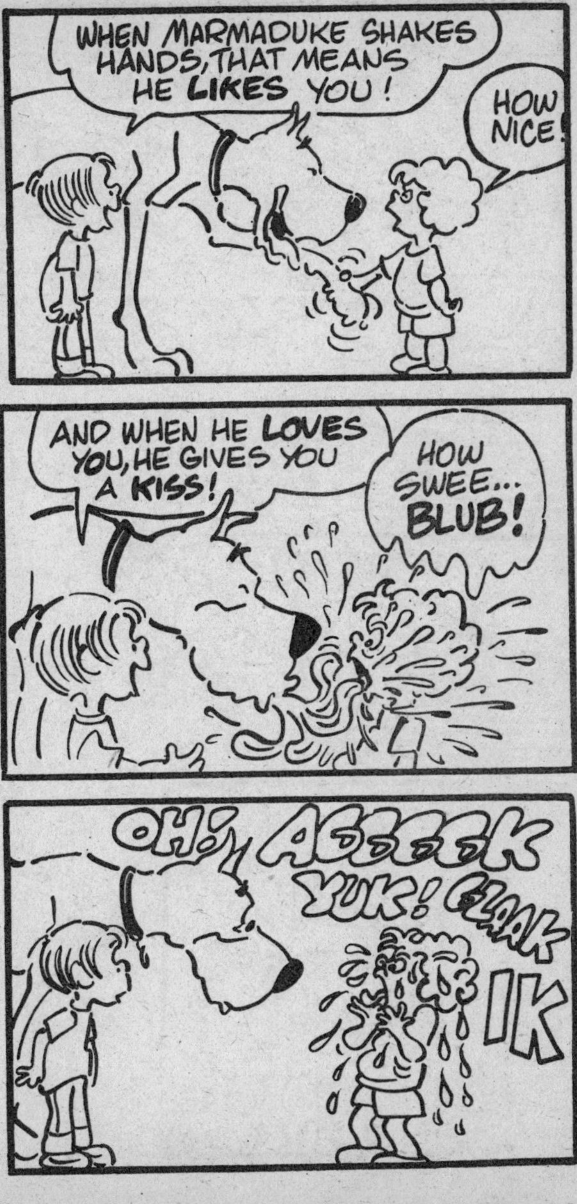
WHEN MARMADUKE SHAKES HANDS, THAT MEANS HE **LIKES** YOU!
HOW NICE!
AND WHEN HE **LOVES** YOU, HE GIVES YOU A **KISS**!
HOW SWEE... **BLUB**!
OH! AGEEEK
YUK! GLAAK
IK

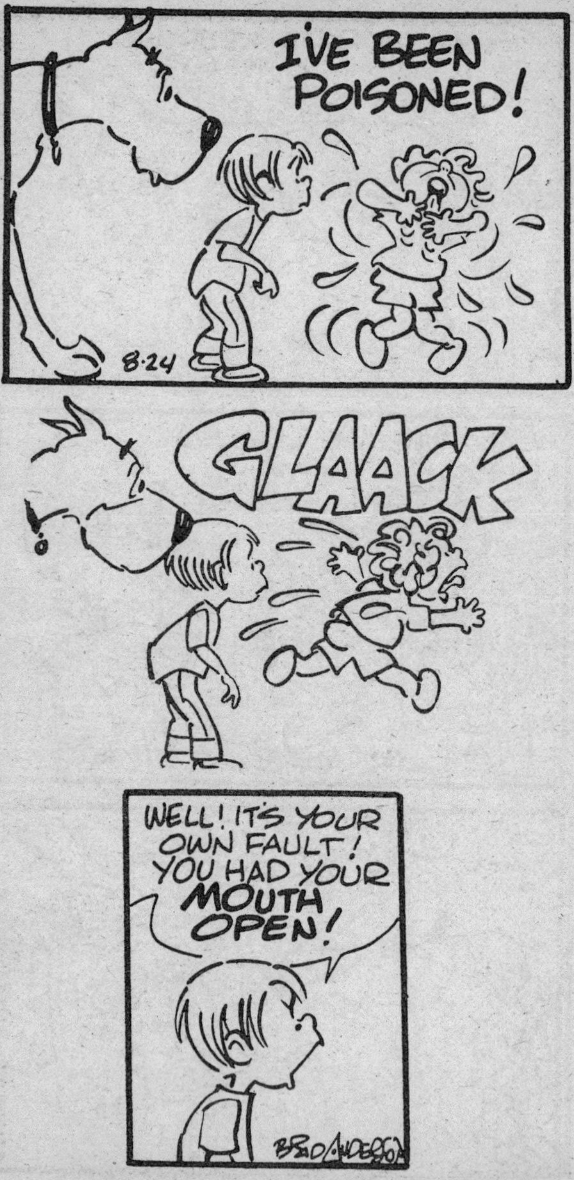
I'VE BEEN POISONED!
8·24
GLAACK
WELL! IT'S YOUR OWN FAULT! YOU HAD YOUR MOUTH OPEN!
BRAD ANDERSON

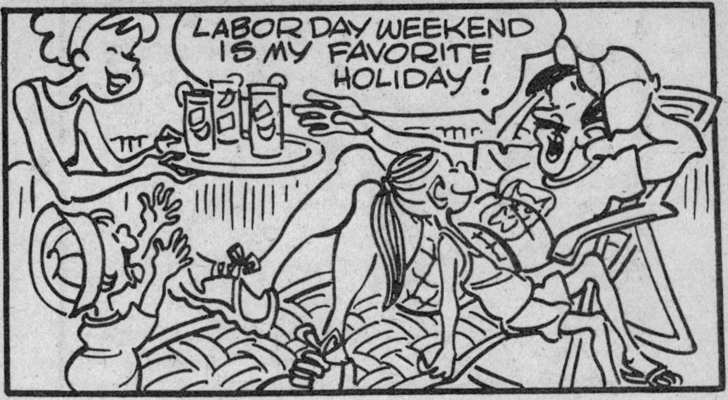
LABOR DAY WEEKEND IS MY FAVORITE HOLIDAY!

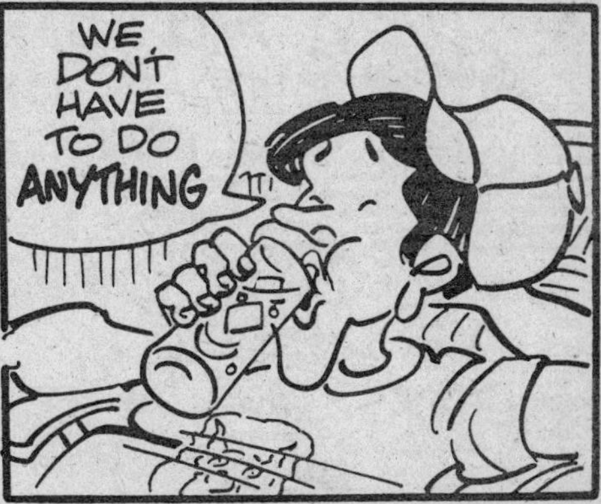
WE DON'T HAVE TO DO ANYTHING

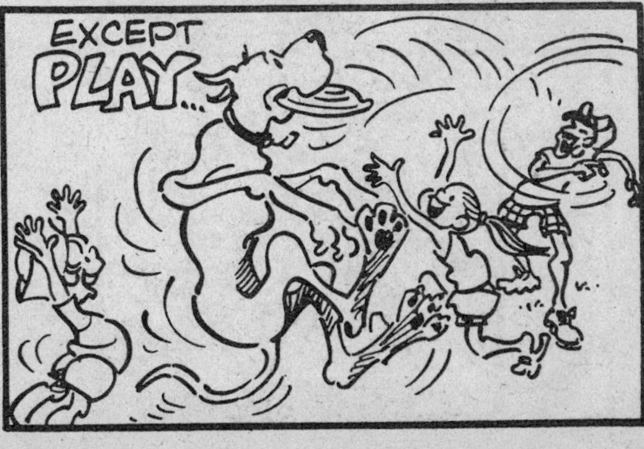
EXCEPT PLAY...

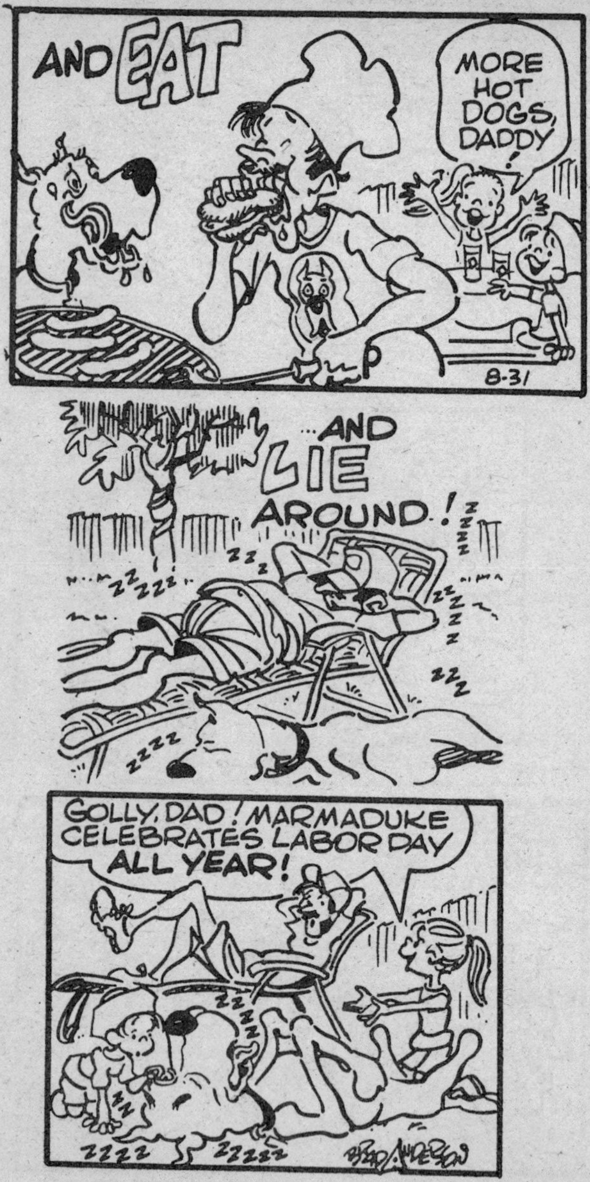
AND EAT
MORE HOT DOGS, DADDY!
8-31
...AND LIE AROUND!
GOLLY, DAD! MARMADUKE CELEBRATES LABOR DAY ALL YEAR!
BRAD ANDERSON

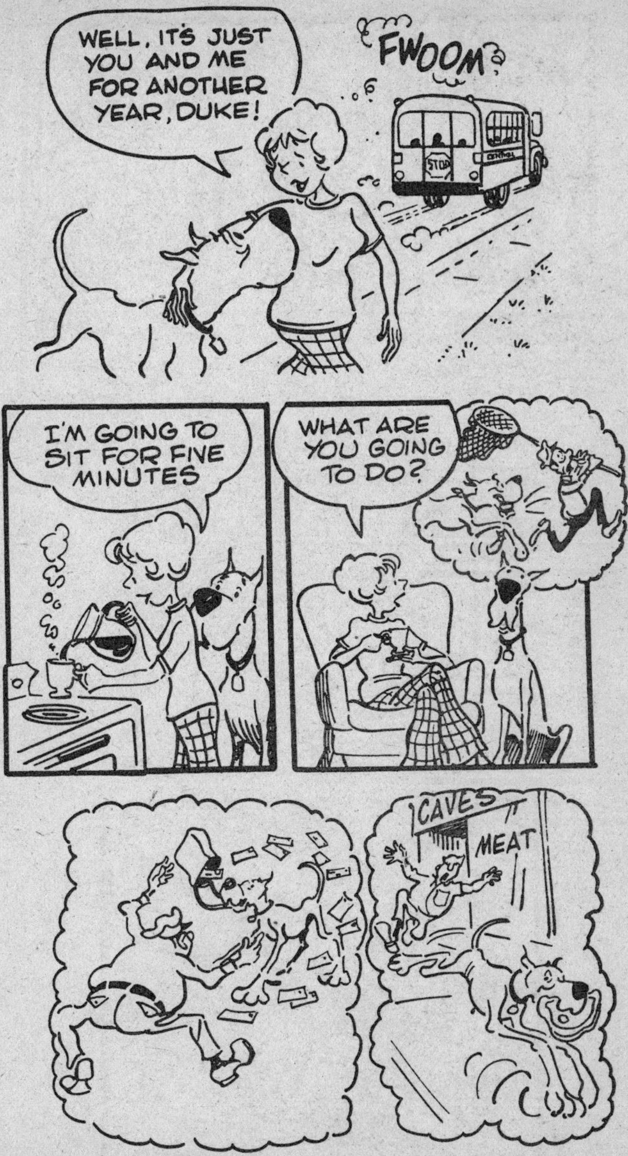
WELL, IT'S JUST YOU AND ME FOR ANOTHER YEAR, DUKE!
FWOOM
STOP
I'M GOING TO SIT FOR FIVE MINUTES
WHAT ARE YOU GOING TO DO?
CAVES
MEAT

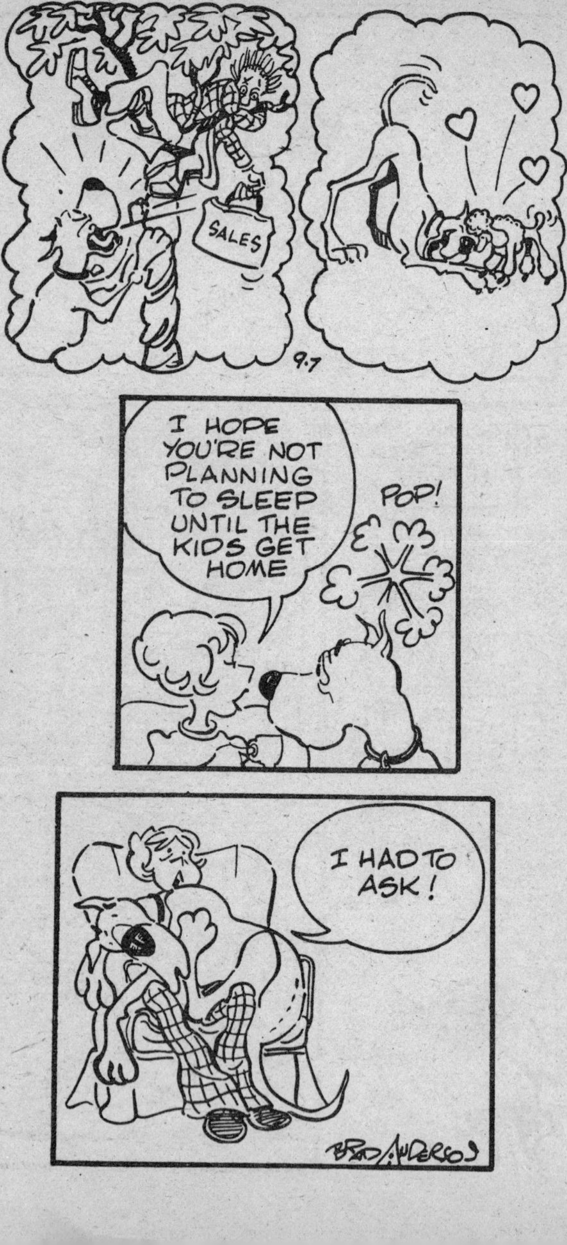
SALES
9-7
I HOPE YOU'RE NOT PLANNING TO SLEEP UNTIL THE KIDS GET HOME
POP!
I HAD TO ASK!
BRAD ANDERSON

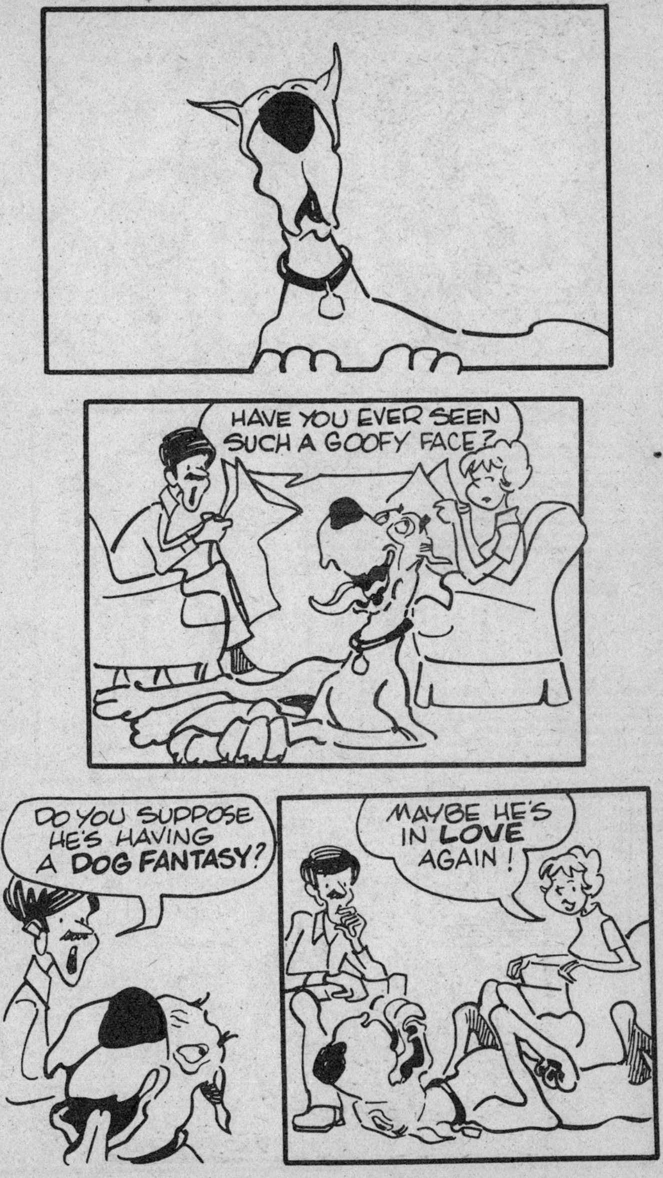
HAVE YOU EVER SEEN SUCH A GOOFY FACE?
DO YOU SUPPOSE HE'S HAVING A **DOG FANTASY**?
MAYBE HE'S IN **LOVE** AGAIN!

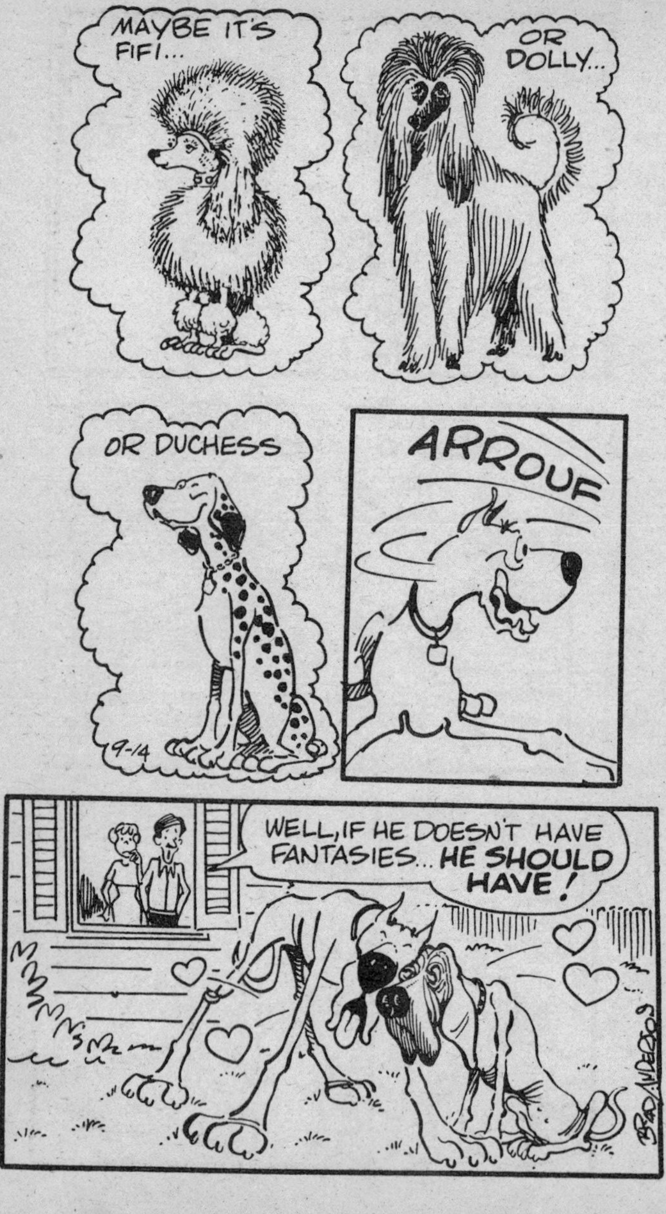
MAYBE IT'S FIFI...
OR DOLLY...
OR DUCHESS
9-14
ARROUF
WELL, IF HE DOESN'T HAVE FANTASIES... **HE SHOULD HAVE!**

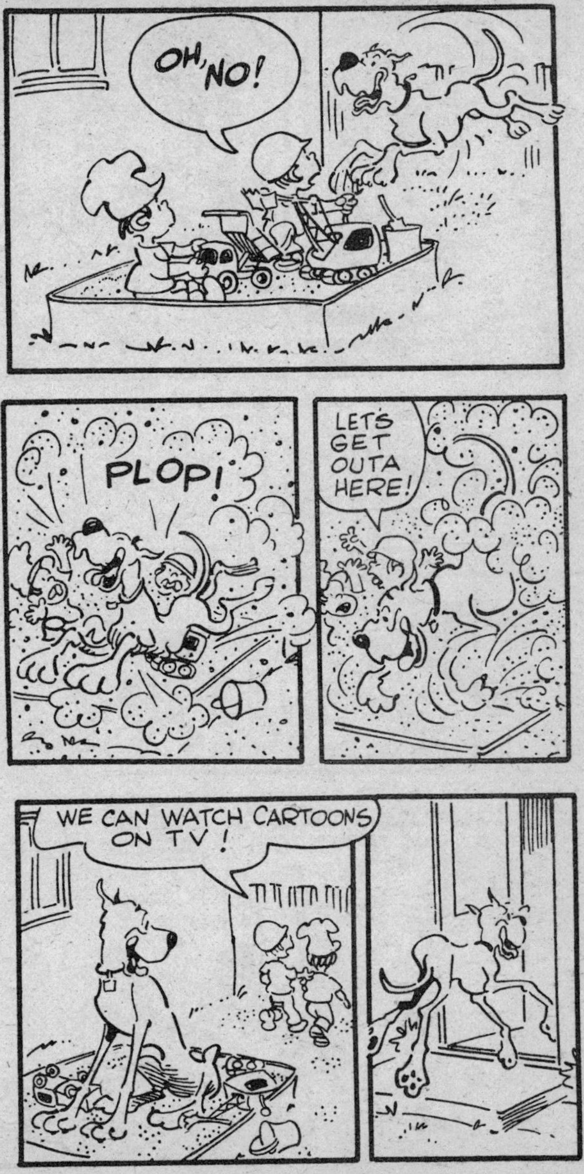
OH, NO!
PLOP!
LETS GET OUTA HERE!
WE CAN WATCH CARTOONS ON TV!

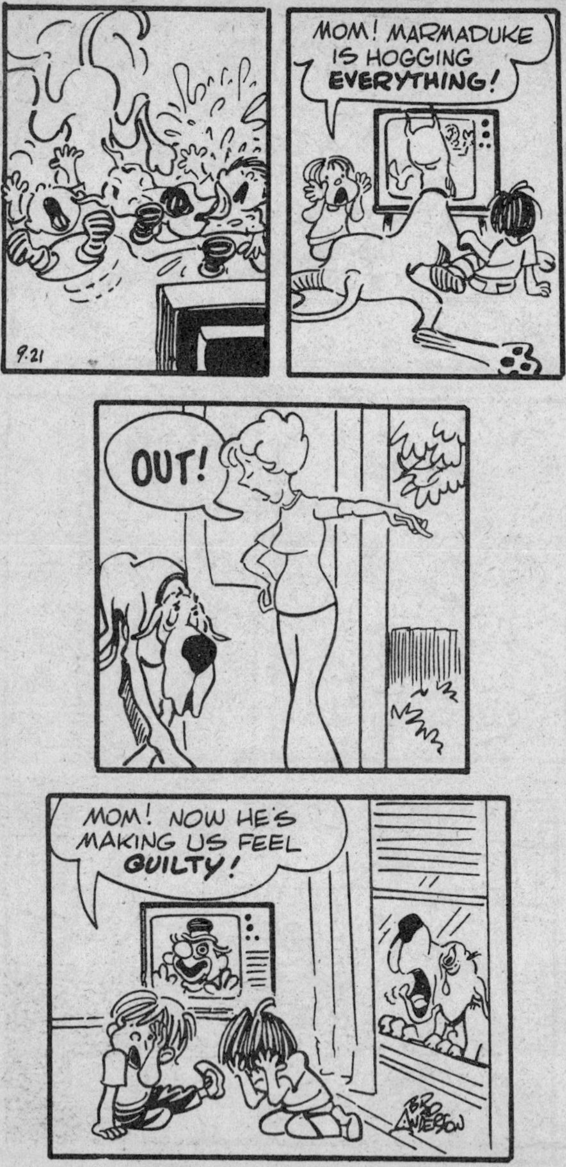
9.21
MOM! MARMADUKE IS HOGGING EVERYTHING!
OUT!
MOM! NOW HE'S MAKING US FEEL GUILTY!
BRAD ANDERSON

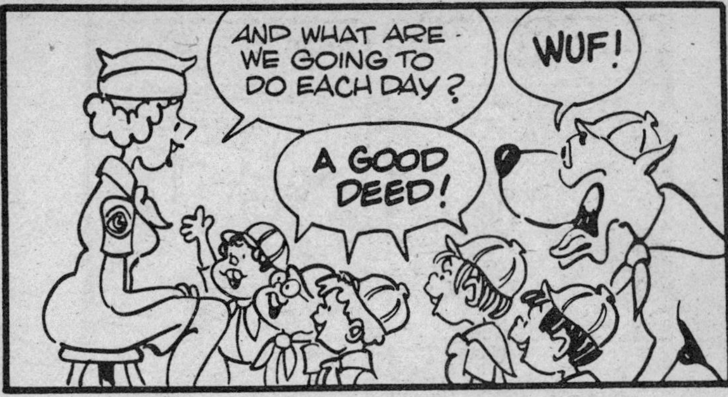
AND WHAT ARE WE GOING TO DO EACH DAY?
WUF!
A GOOD DEED!

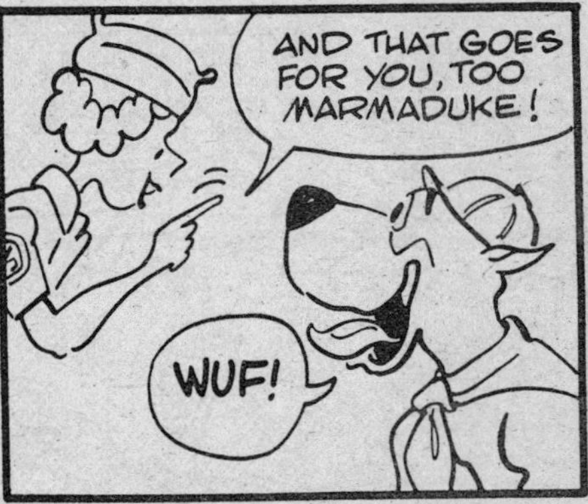
AND THAT GOES FOR YOU, TOO MARMADUKE!
WUF!

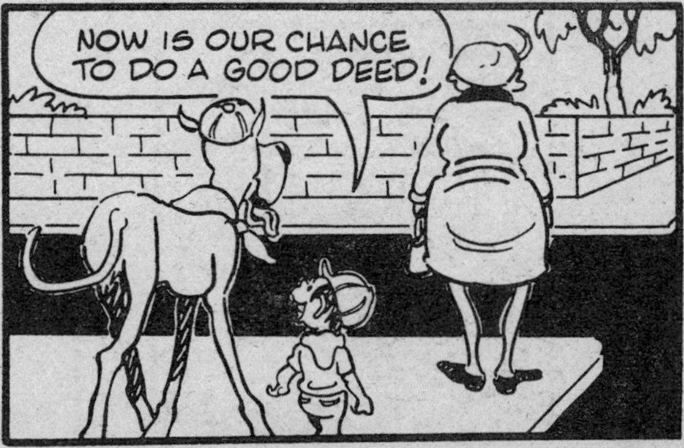
NOW IS OUR CHANCE TO DO A GOOD DEED!

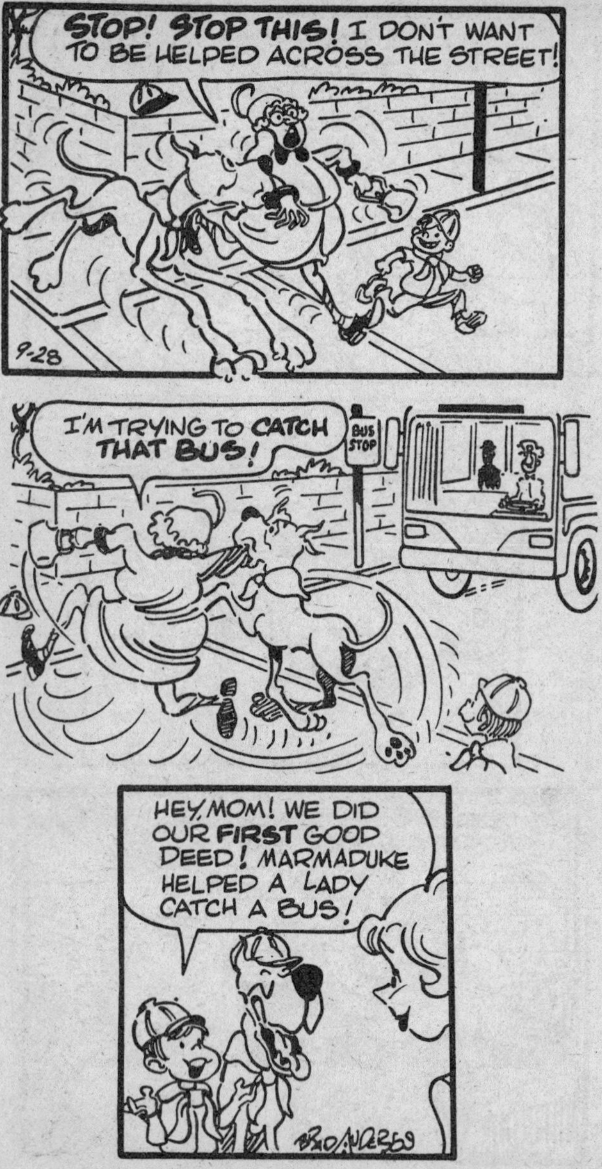
STOP! STOP THIS! I DON'T WANT TO BE HELPED ACROSS THE STREET!
9-28
I'M TRYING TO CATCH THAT BUS!
BUS STOP
HEY, MOM! WE DID OUR FIRST GOOD DEED! MARMADUKE HELPED A LADY CATCH A BUS!

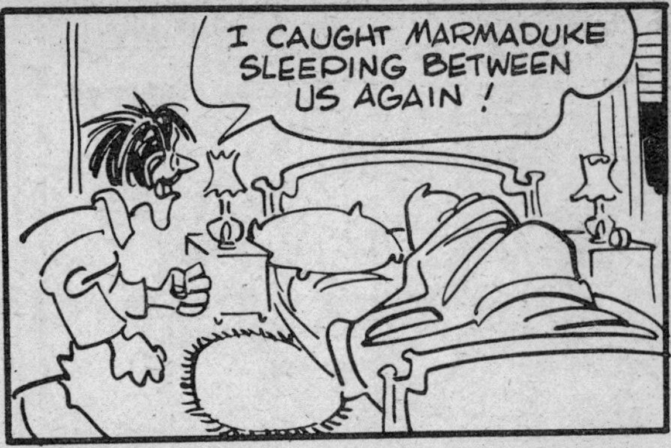
I CAUGHT MARMADUKE SLEEPING BETWEEN US AGAIN !

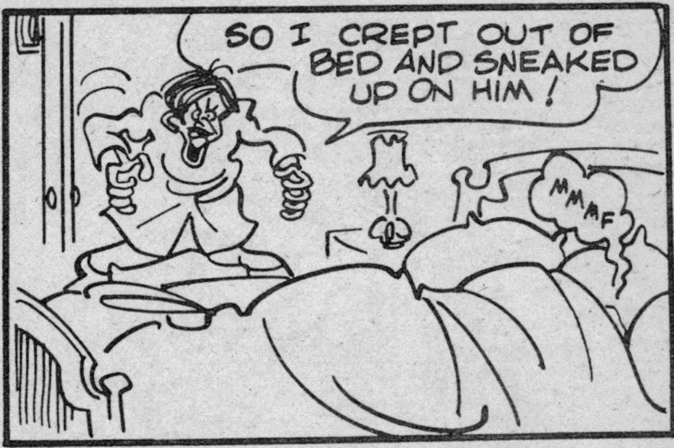
SO I CREPT OUT OF BED AND SNEAKED UP ON HIM !
MMMF

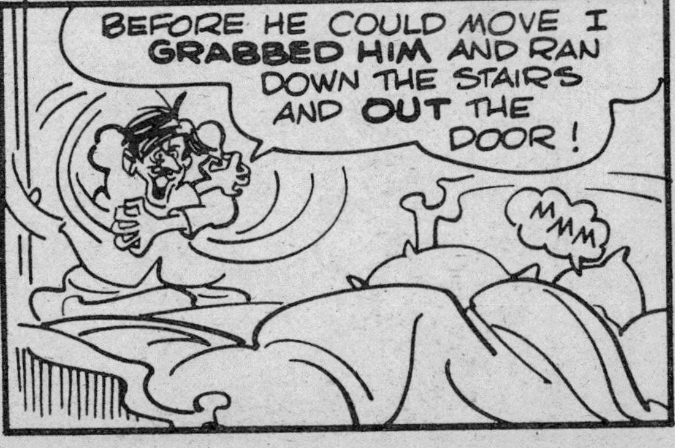
BEFORE HE COULD MOVE I **GRABBED HIM** AND RAN DOWN THE STAIRS AND **OUT** THE DOOR !
MMM

WHAT A FIGHT HE PUT UP! KICKING! THRASHING! HOWLING!
THEN WITH ONE MIGHTY HEAVE...
I STUFFED HIM IN HIS DOGHOUSE!
HAR! HAR!
OH, NO!
MMGF
10·5
BRAD ANDERSON

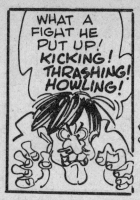

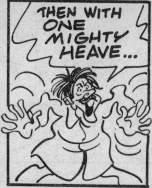

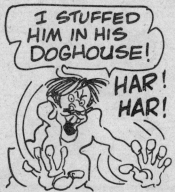

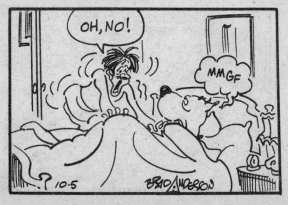

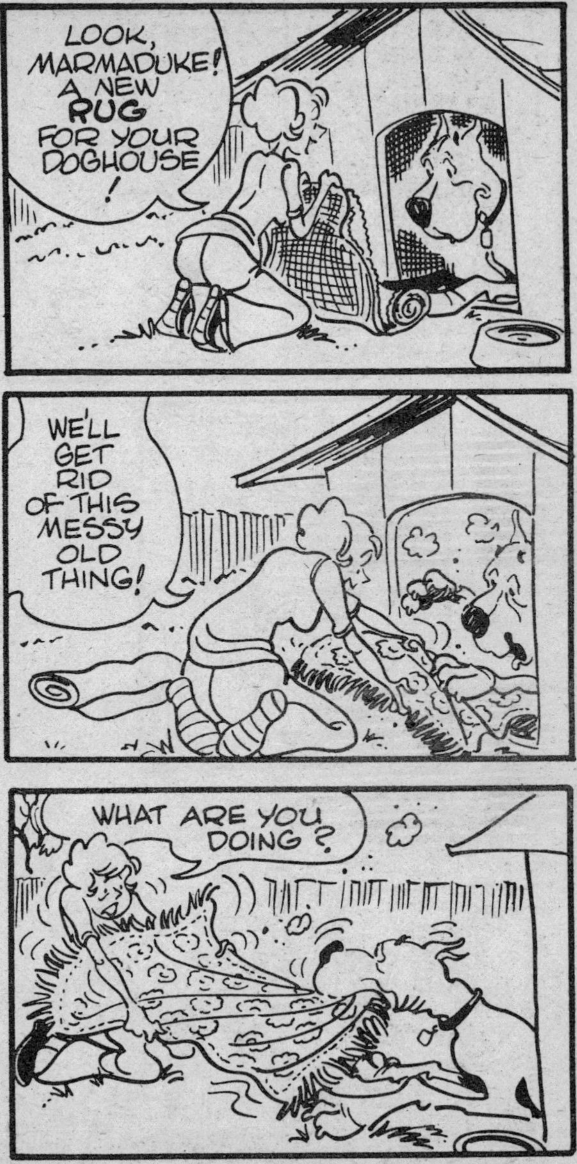
LOOK, MARMADUKE! A NEW RUG FOR YOUR DOGHOUSE!
WE'LL GET RID OF THIS MESSY OLD THING!
WHAT ARE YOU DOING?

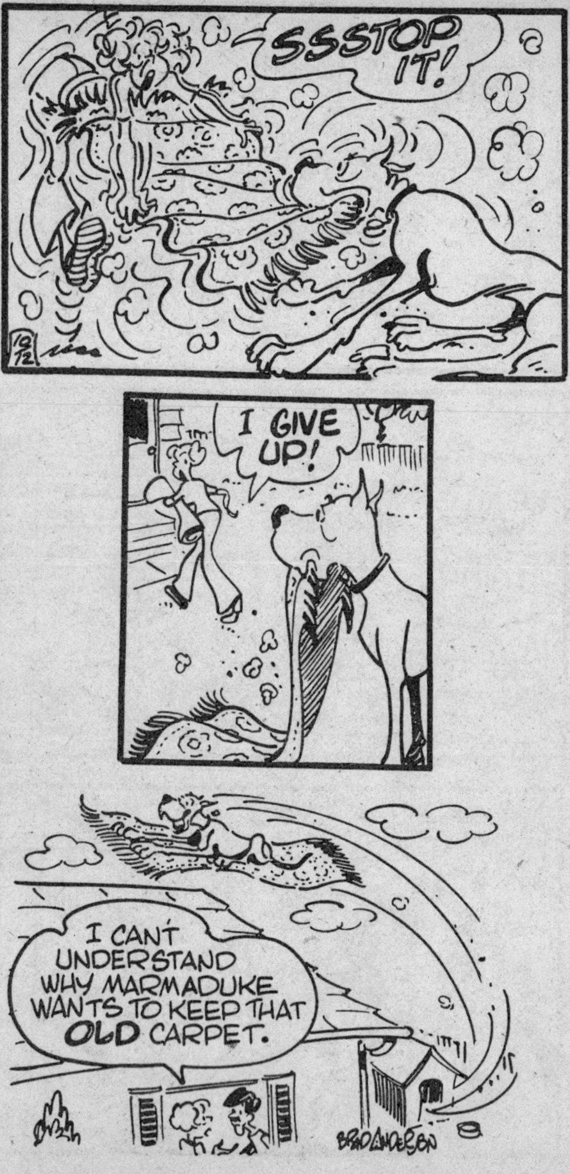
SSSTOP IT!
10/12
I GIVE UP!
I CAN'T UNDERSTAND WHY MARMADUKE WANTS TO KEEP THAT OLD CARPET.
BRAD ANDERSON

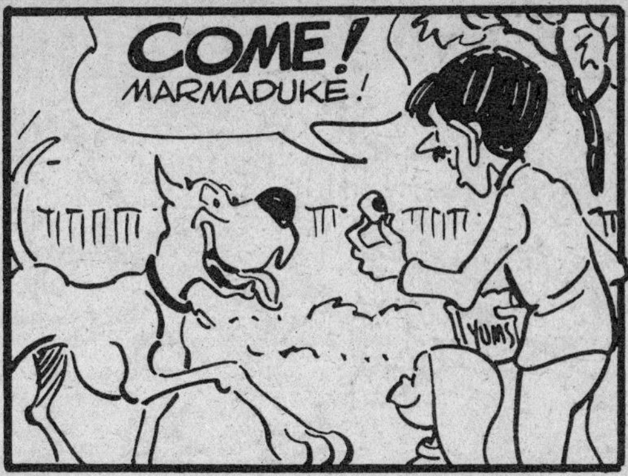
COME! MARMADUKE!
YUMS

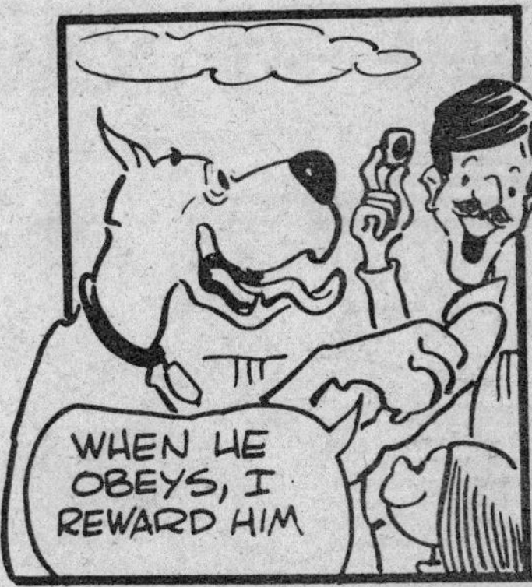
WHEN HE OBEYS, I REWARD HIM

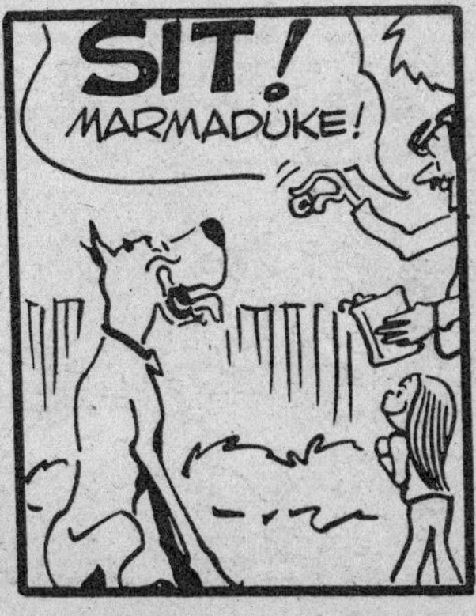
SIT! MARMADUKE!

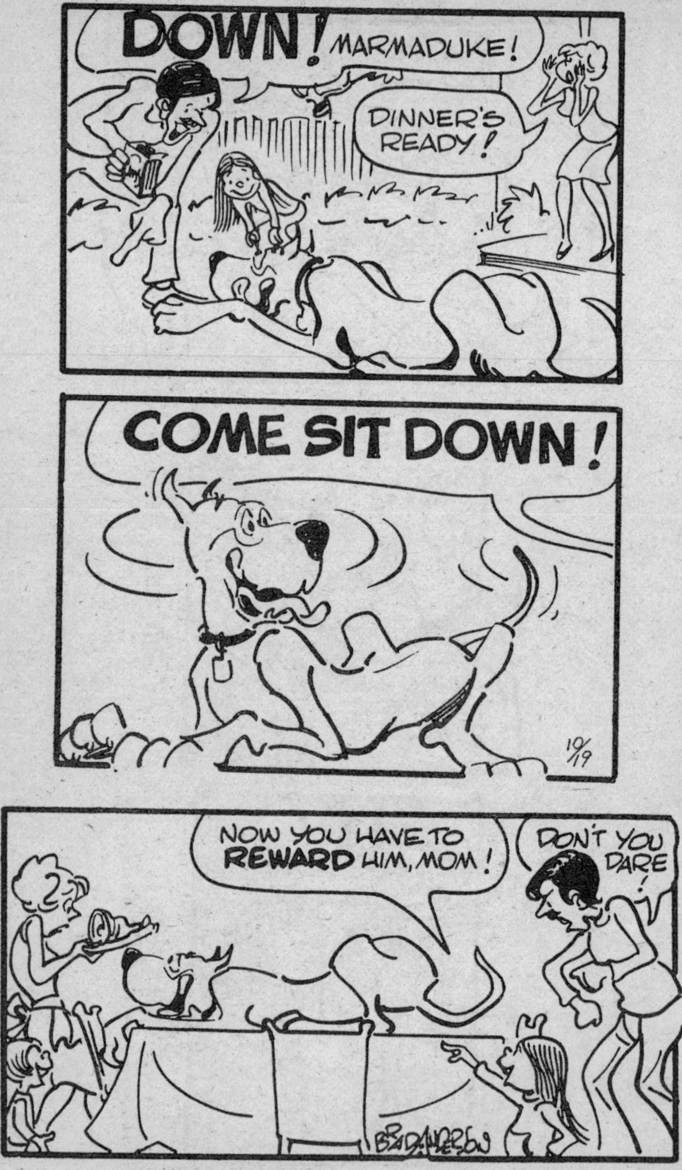
DOWN! MARMADUKE!
DINNER'S READY!
COME SIT DOWN!
10/19
NOW YOU HAVE TO REWARD HIM, MOM!
DON'T YOU DARE!
BRAD ANDERSON

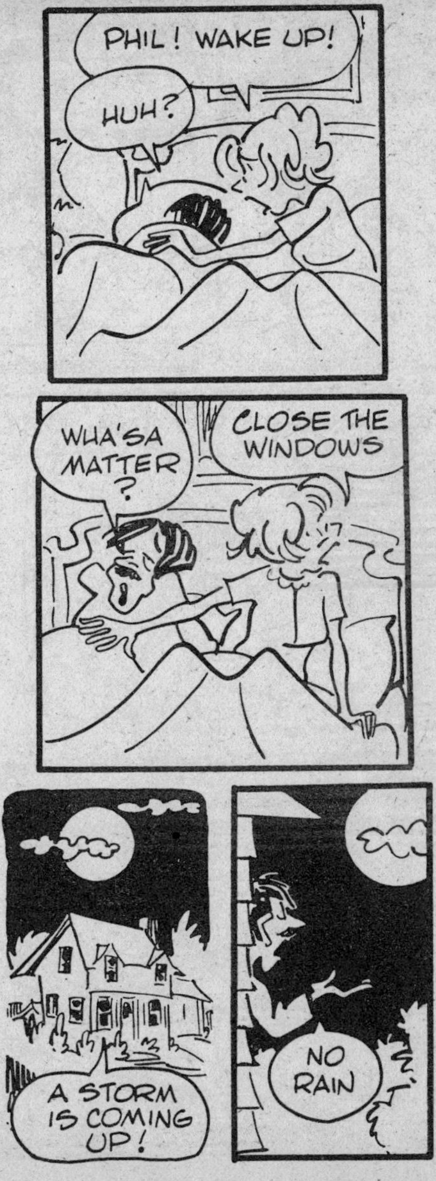
PHIL! WAKE UP!
HUH?
WHA'SA MATTER?
CLOSE THE WINDOWS
A STORM IS COMING UP!
NO RAIN

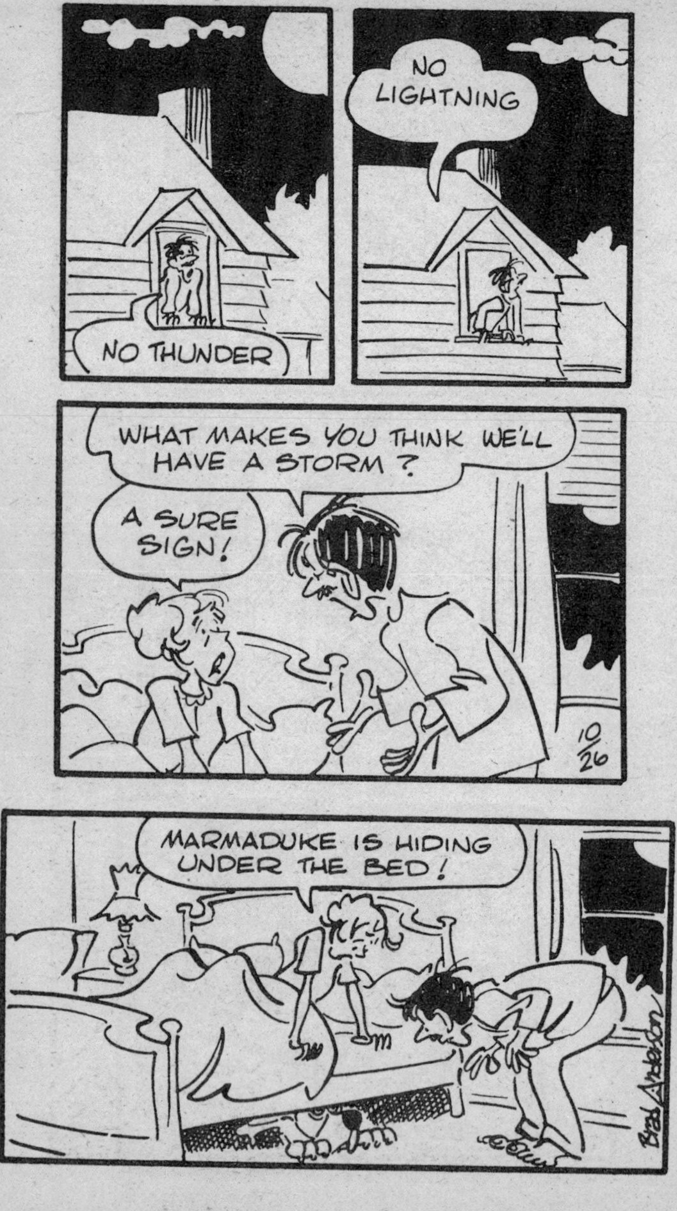
NO THUNDER
NO LIGHTNING
WHAT MAKES YOU THINK WE'LL HAVE A STORM?
A SURE SIGN!
10/26
MARMADUKE IS HIDING UNDER THE BED!
Brad Anderson

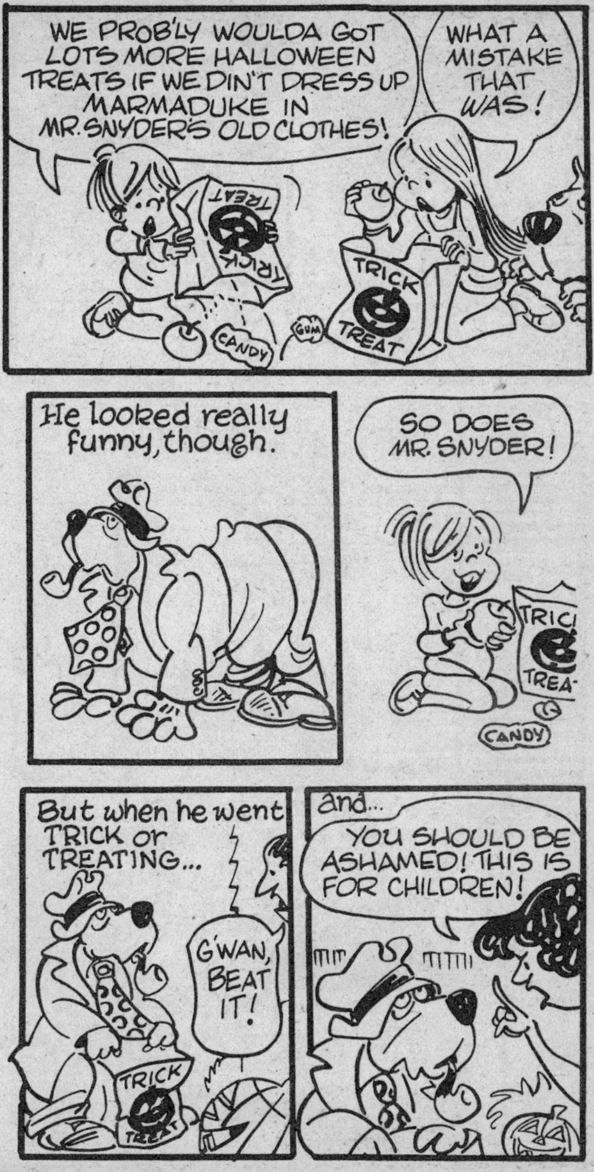
WE PROB'LY WOULDA GOT LOTS MORE HALLOWEEN TREATS IF WE DIN'T DRESS UP MARMADUKE IN MR. SNYDER'S OLD CLOTHES!
WHAT A MISTAKE THAT WAS!
TRICK TREAT
TRICK TREAT
CANDY
GUM
He looked really funny, though.
SO DOES MR. SNYDER!
TRICK TREAT
CANDY
But when he went TRICK or TREATING...
G'WAN, BEAT IT!
TRICK TREAT
and...
YOU SHOULD BE ASHAMED! THIS IS FOR CHILDREN!

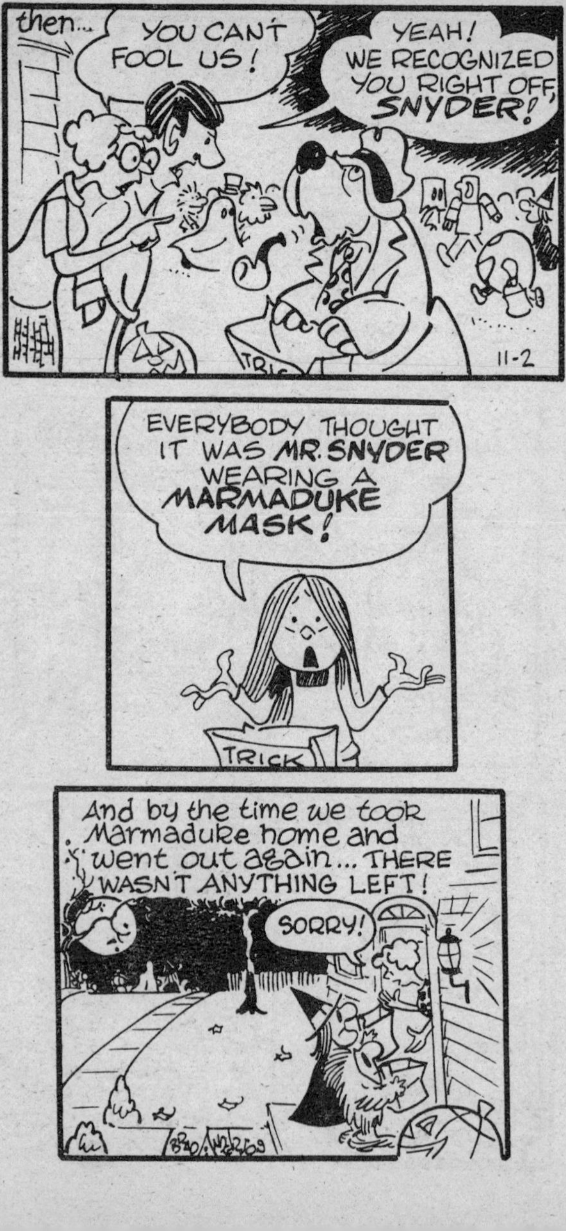
then...
YOU CAN'T FOOL US!
YEAH! WE RECOGNIZED YOU RIGHT OFF, SNYDER!
11-2
EVERYBODY THOUGHT IT WAS MR. SNYDER WEARING A MARMADUKE MASK!
TRICK
And by the time we took Marmaduke home and went out again... THERE WASN'T ANYTHING LEFT!
SORRY!

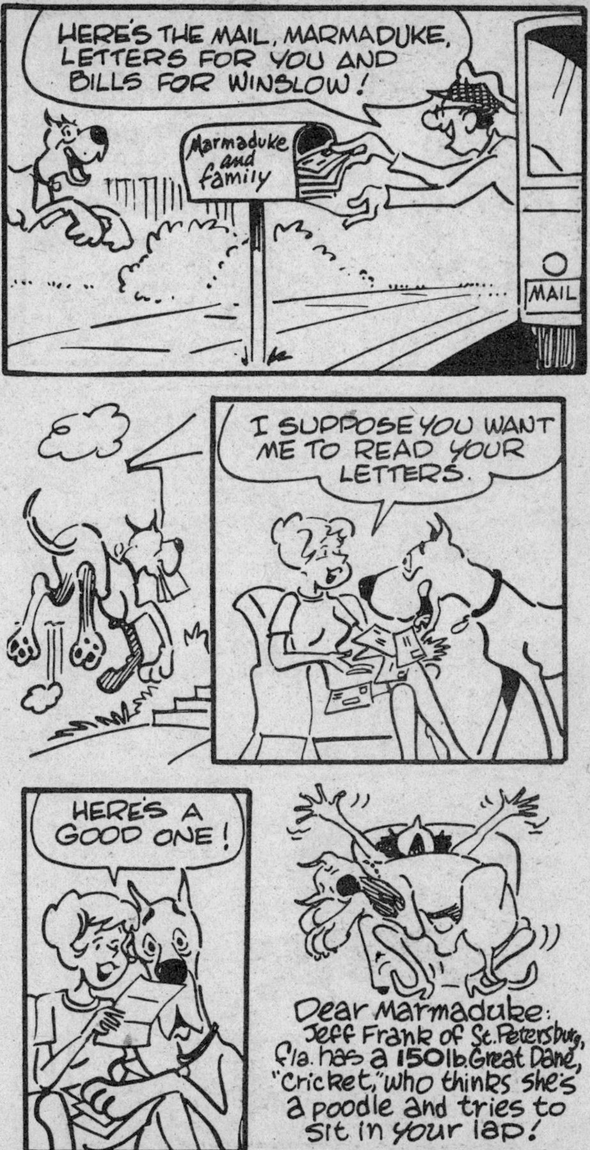
HERE'S THE MAIL, MARMADUKE, LETTERS FOR YOU AND BILLS FOR WINSLOW!
Marmaduke and family
MAIL
I SUPPOSE YOU WANT ME TO READ YOUR LETTERS.
HERE'S A GOOD ONE!
Dear Marmaduke:
Jeff Frank of St. Petersburg, Fla. has a 150 lb. Great Dane, "Cricket," who thinks she's a poodle and tries to sit in your lap!

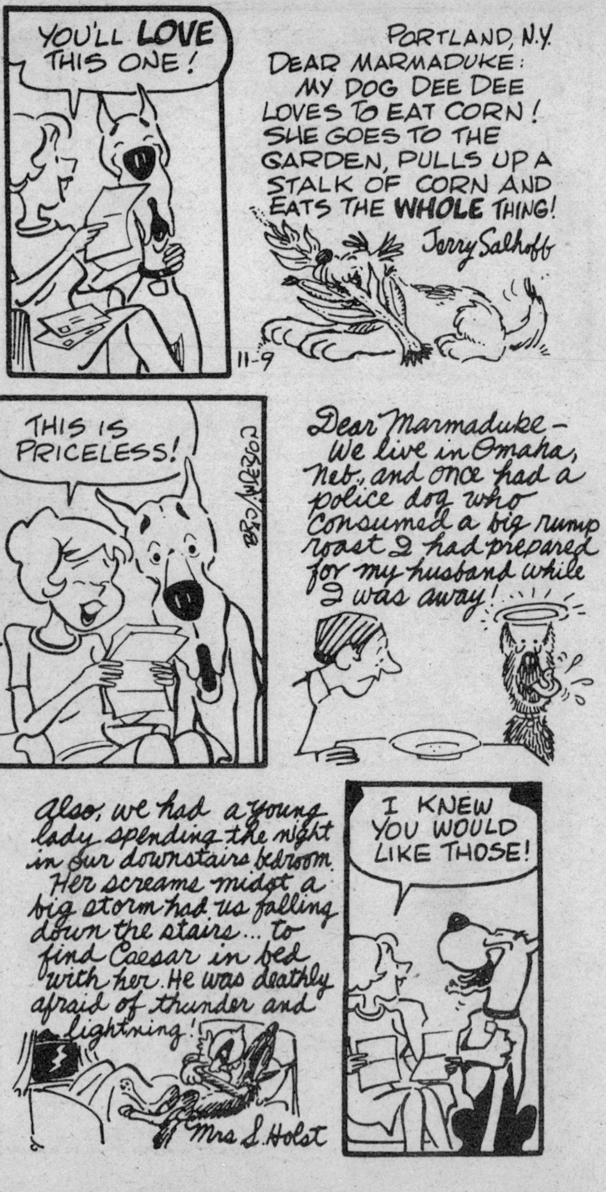
YOU'LL **LOVE** THIS ONE!
PORTLAND, N.Y.
DEAR MARMADUKE:
MY DOG DEE DEE LOVES TO EAT CORN! SHE GOES TO THE GARDEN, PULLS UP A STALK OF CORN AND EATS THE **WHOLE** THING!
Jerry Salhoff
11-9
THIS IS PRICELESS!
Dear Marmaduke -
We live in Omaha, Neb., and once had a police dog who consumed a big rump roast I had prepared for my husband while I was away!
Also, we had a young lady spending the night in our downstairs bedroom. Her screams midst a big storm had us falling down the stairs... to find Caesar in bed with her. He was deathly afraid of thunder and lightning!
Mrs. S. Holst
I KNEW YOU WOULD LIKE THOSE!

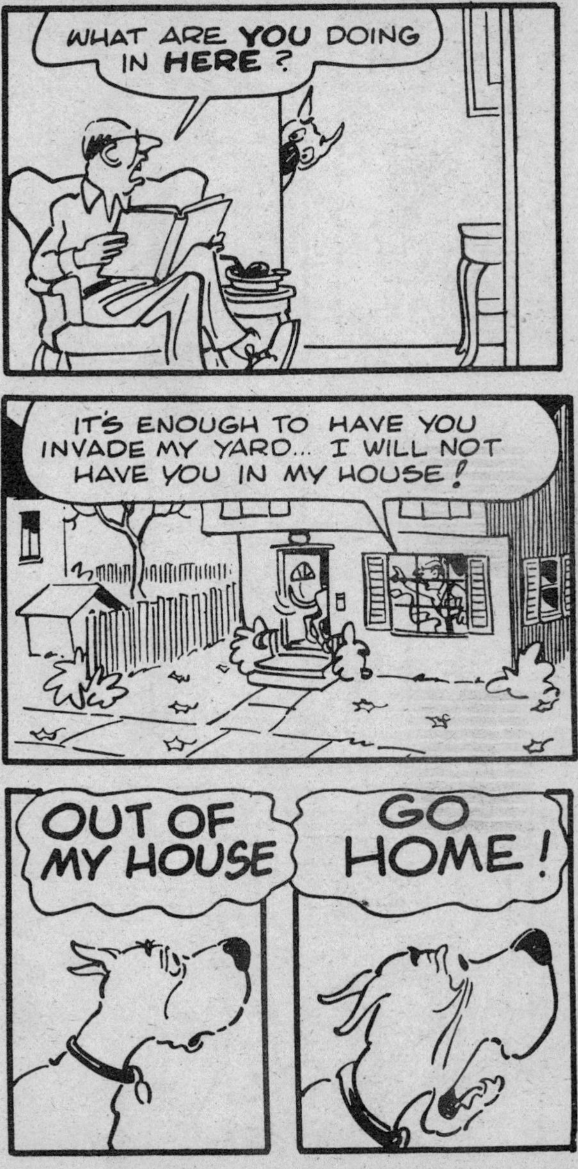
WHAT ARE YOU DOING IN HERE ?
IT'S ENOUGH TO HAVE YOU INVADE MY YARD... I WILL NOT HAVE YOU IN MY HOUSE !
OUT OF MY HOUSE
GO HOME !

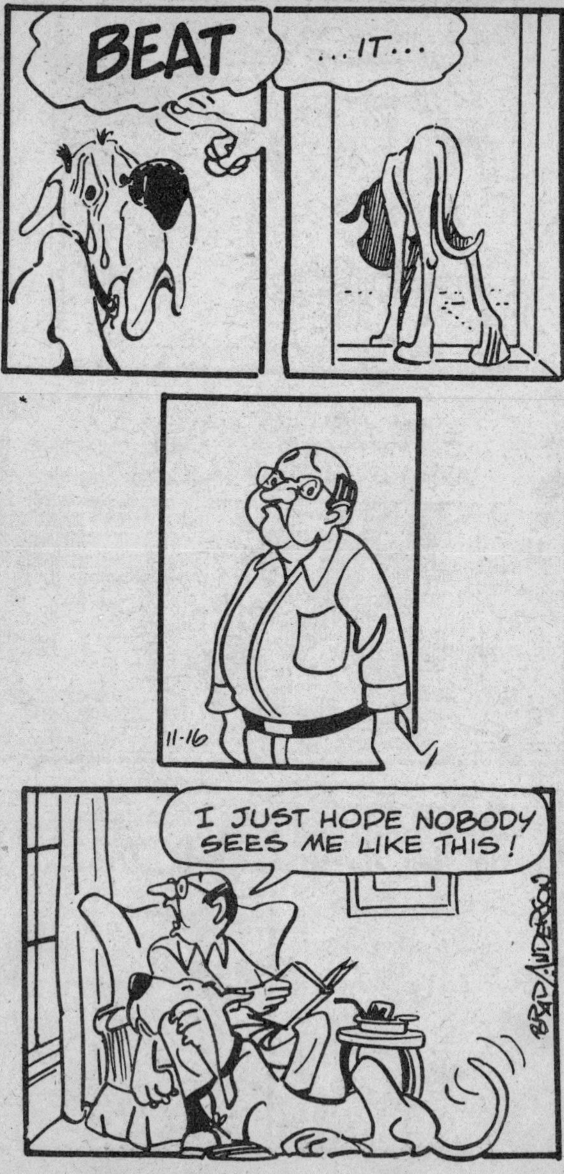
BEAT
...IT...
11-16
I JUST HOPE NOBODY SEES ME LIKE THIS!
BRAD ANDERSON

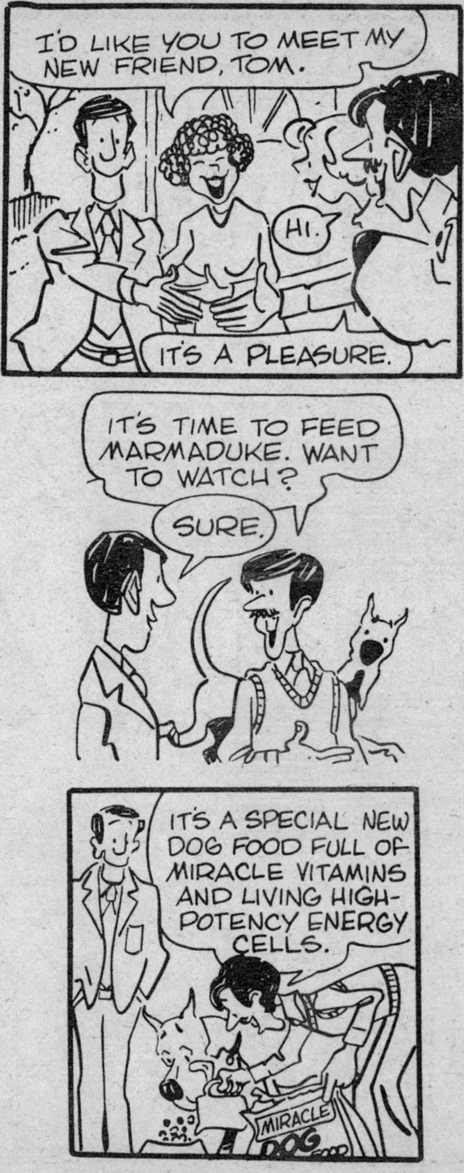
I'D LIKE YOU TO MEET MY NEW FRIEND, TOM.
HI.
IT'S A PLEASURE.
IT'S TIME TO FEED MARMADUKE. WANT TO WATCH?
SURE.
IT'S A SPECIAL NEW DOG FOOD FULL OF MIRACLE VITAMINS AND LIVING HIGH-POTENCY ENERGY CELLS.
MIRACLE
DOG

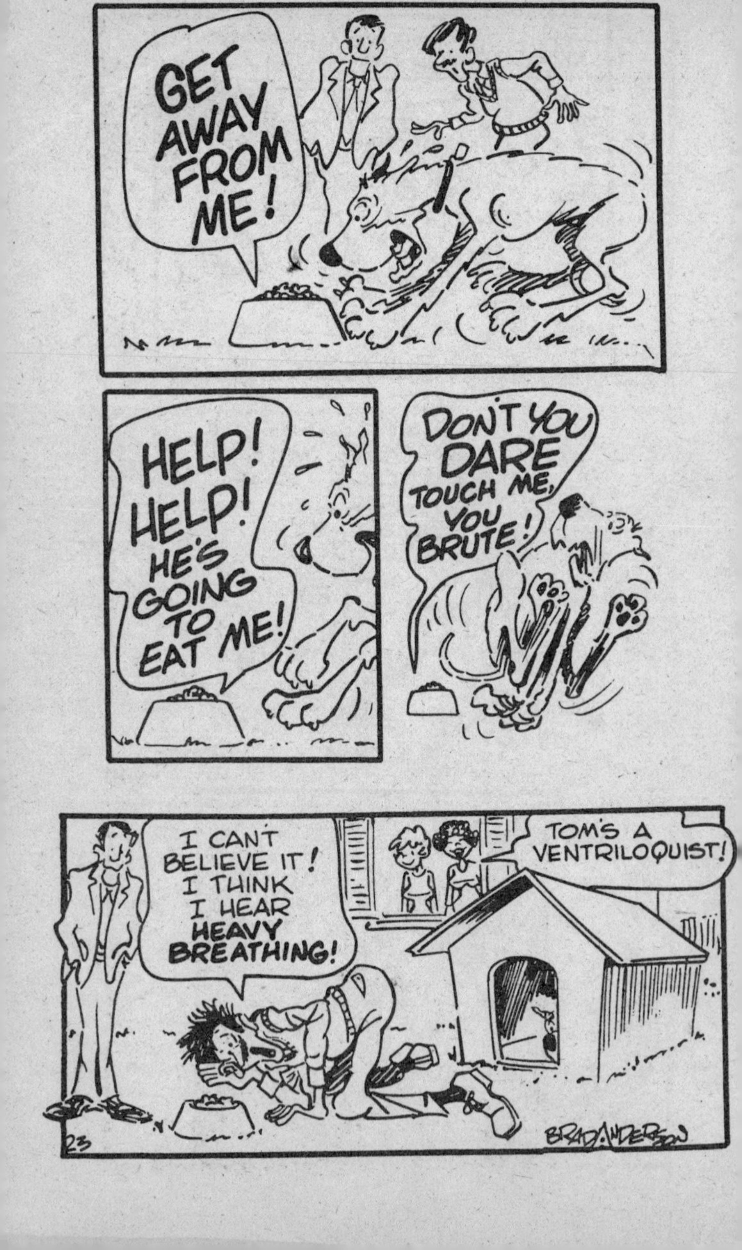
GET AWAY FROM ME!
HELP! HELP! HE'S GOING TO EAT ME!
DON'T YOU DARE TOUCH ME, YOU BRUTE!
I CAN'T BELIEVE IT! I THINK I HEAR HEAVY BREATHING!
TOM'S A VENTRILOQUIST!
BRAD ANDERSON
23

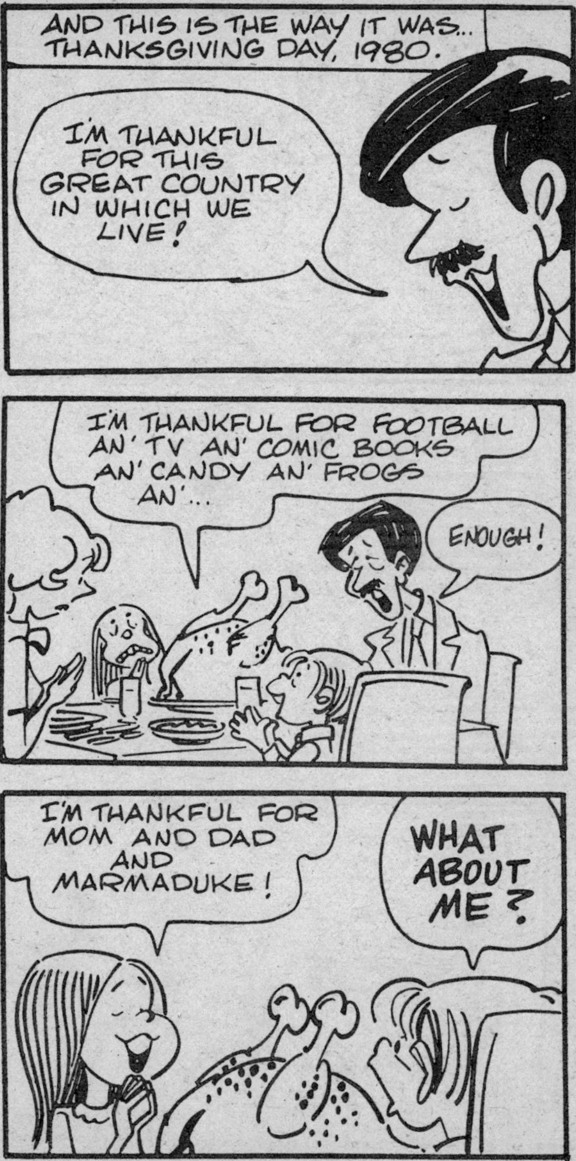
AND THIS IS THE WAY IT WAS... THANKSGIVING DAY, 1980.
I'M THANKFUL FOR THIS GREAT COUNTRY IN WHICH WE LIVE!
I'M THANKFUL FOR FOOTBALL AN' TV AN' COMIC BOOKS AN' CANDY AN' FROGS AN'...
ENOUGH!
I'M THANKFUL FOR MOM AND DAD AND MARMADUKE!
WHAT ABOUT ME?

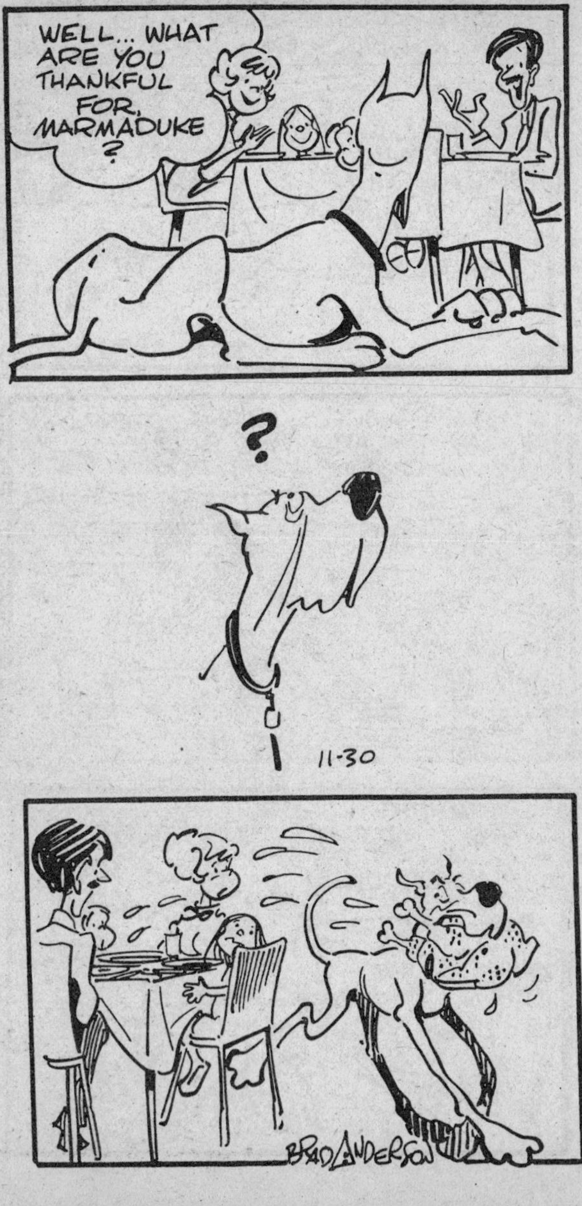
WELL... WHAT ARE YOU THANKFUL FOR, MARMADUKE ?
?
11-30
BRAD ANDERSON

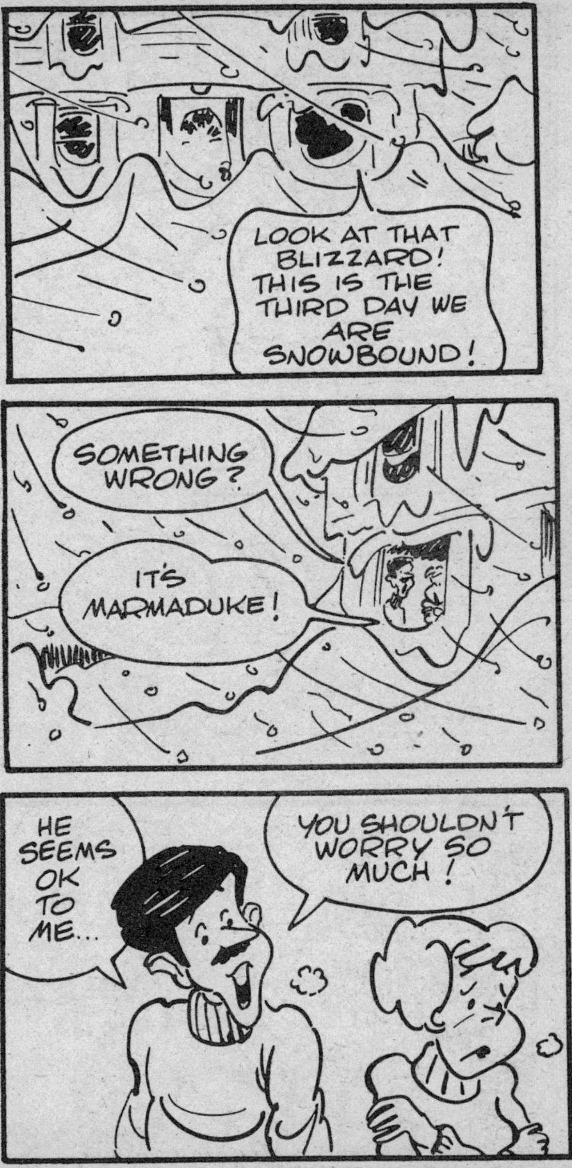
LOOK AT THAT BLIZZARD! THIS IS THE THIRD DAY WE ARE SNOWBOUND!
SOMETHING WRONG?
IT'S MARMADUKE!
HE SEEMS OK TO ME...
YOU SHOULDN'T WORRY SO MUCH!

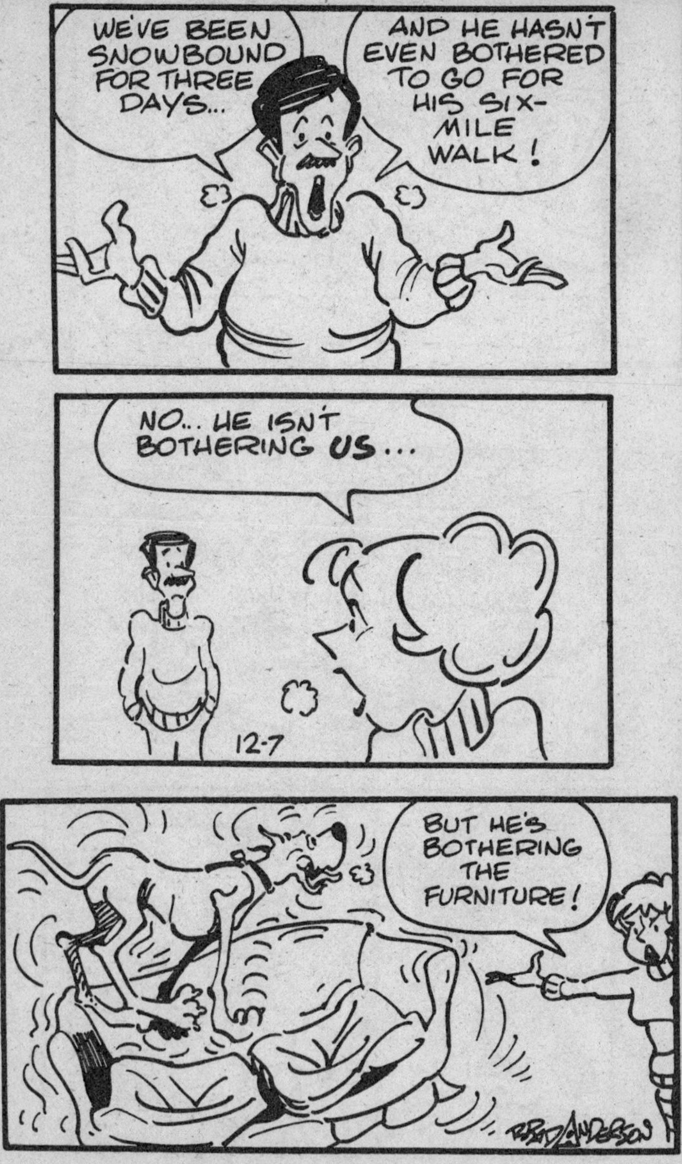
WE'VE BEEN SNOWBOUND FOR THREE DAYS...
AND HE HASN'T EVEN BOTHERED TO GO FOR HIS SIX-MILE WALK!
NO... HE ISN'T BOTHERING US...
12-7
BUT HE'S BOTHERING THE FURNITURE!
BRAD ANDERSON

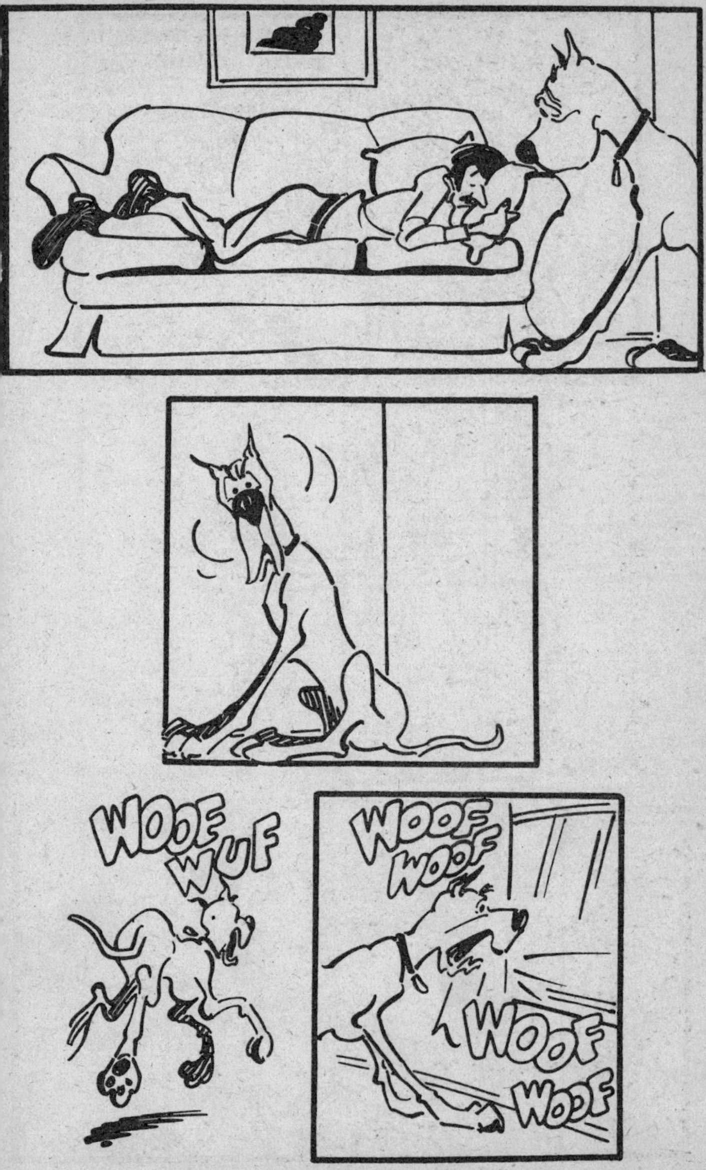
WOOF WUF
WOOF WOOF
WOOF
WOOF

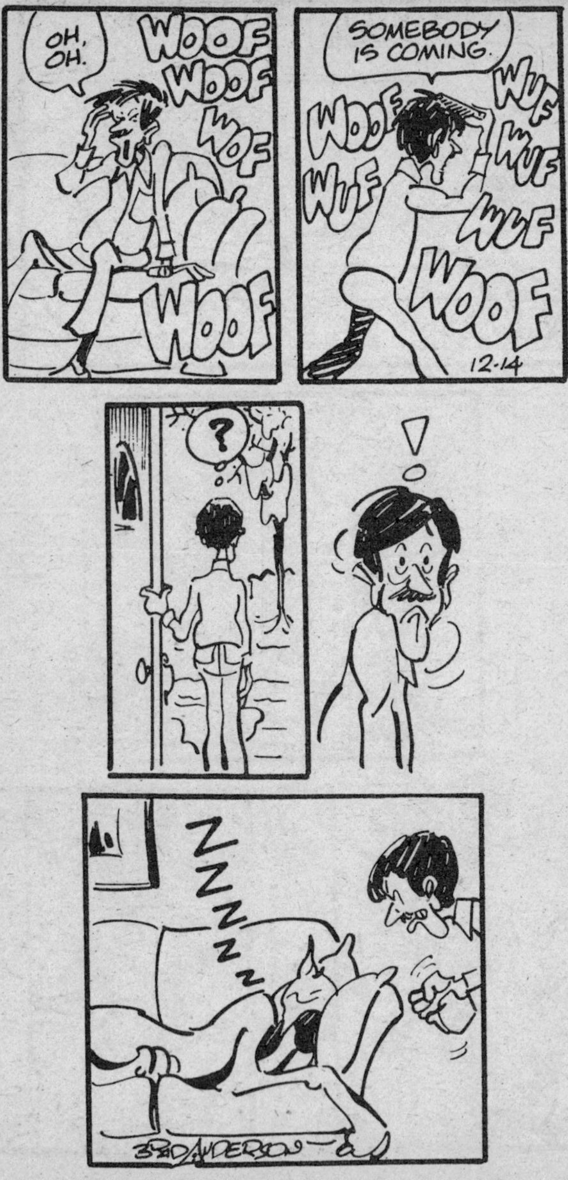
OH, OH.
WOOF
WOOF
WUF
WOOF
SOMEBODY IS COMING.
WOOF
WUF
WUF
WUF
WUF
WOOF
12-14
?
!
ZZZZZ
BRAD ANDERSON

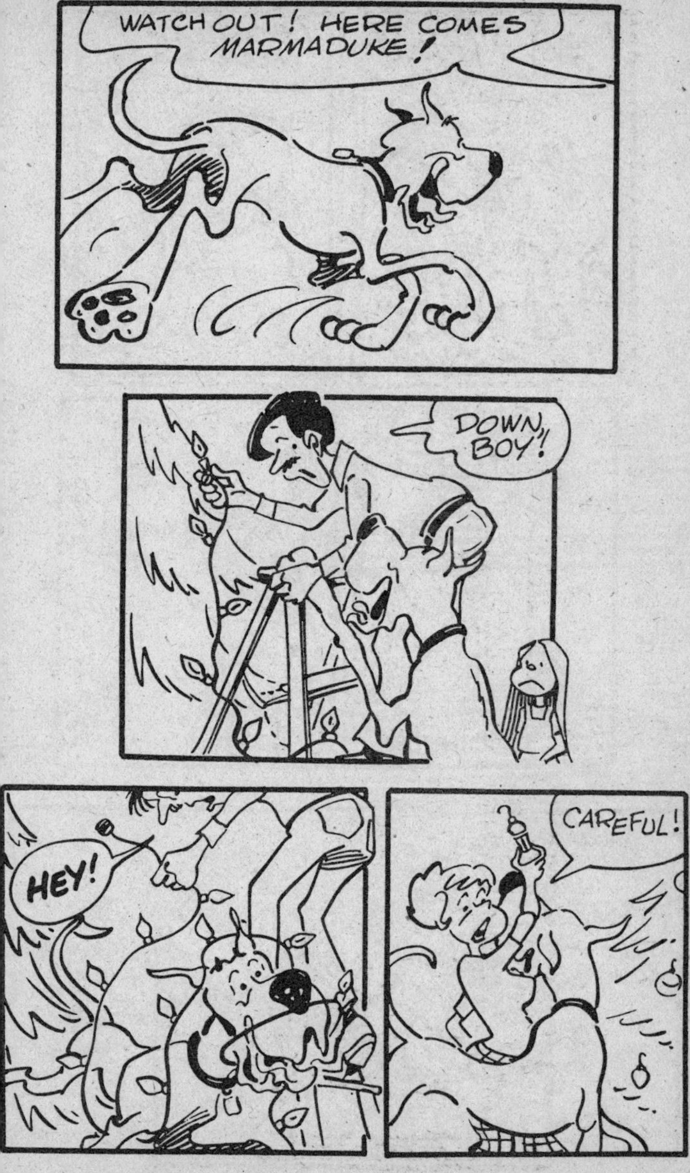
WATCH OUT! HERE COMES MARMADUKE!
DOWN, BOY!
HEY!
CAREFUL!

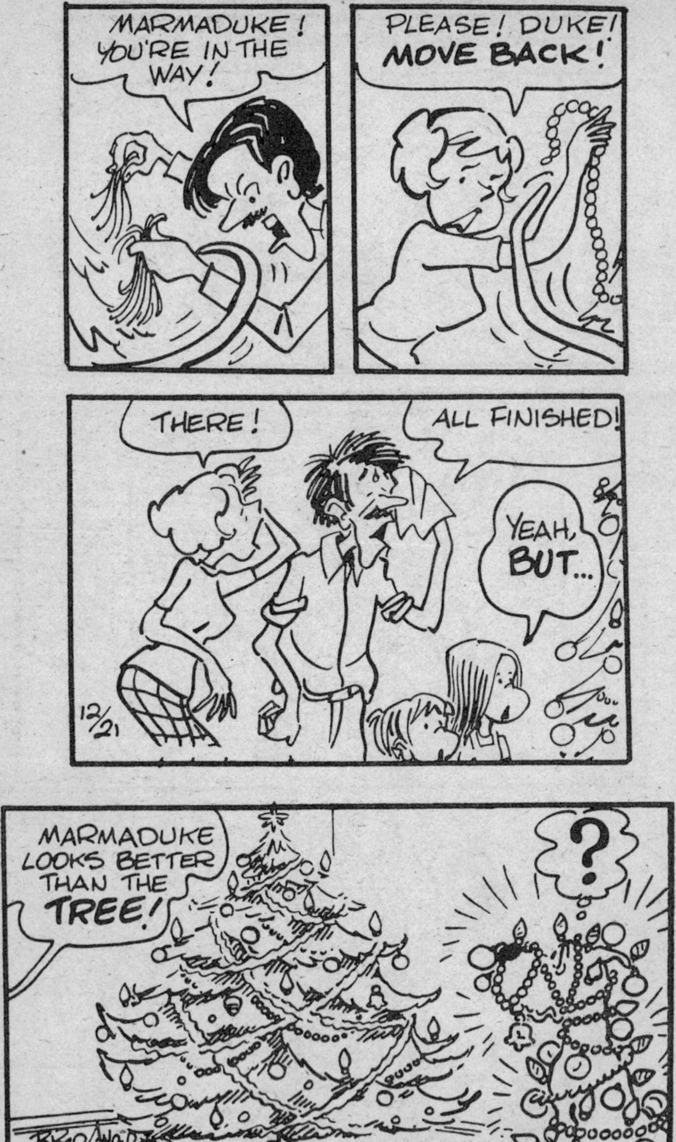
MARMADUKE! YOU'RE IN THE WAY!
PLEASE! DUKE! MOVE BACK!
THERE!
ALL FINISHED!
YEAH, BUT...
12/21
MARMADUKE LOOKS BETTER THAN THE TREE!
?

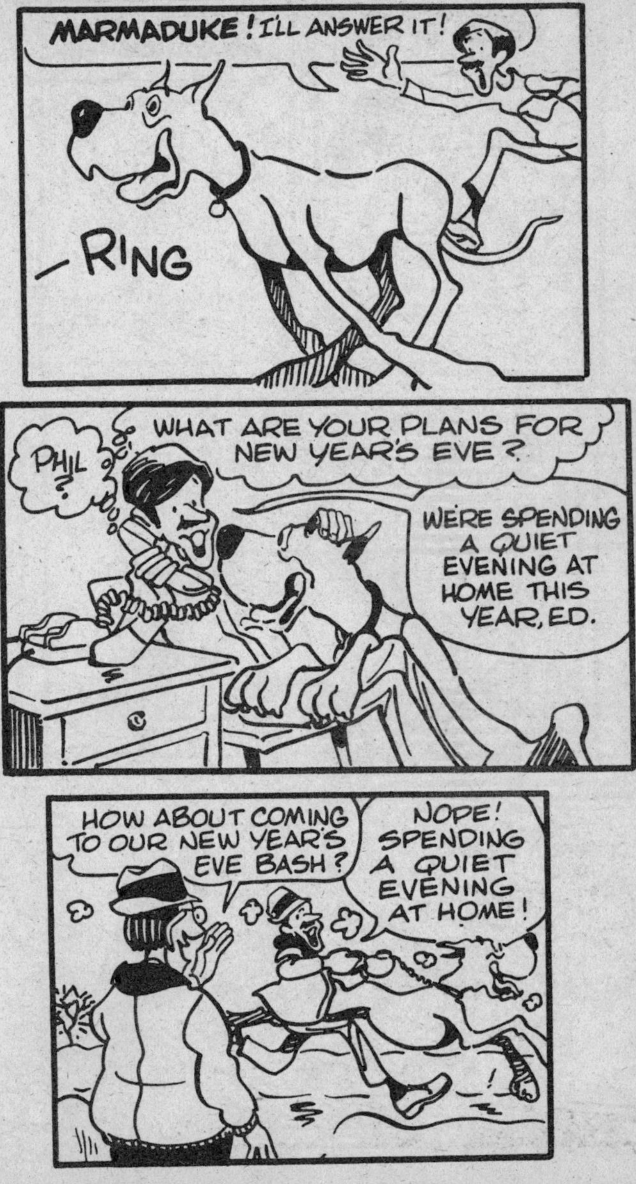
MARMADUKE! I'LL ANSWER IT!
—RING
PHIL ?
WHAT ARE YOUR PLANS FOR NEW YEAR'S EVE ?
WE'RE SPENDING A QUIET EVENING AT HOME THIS YEAR, ED.
HOW ABOUT COMING TO OUR NEW YEAR'S EVE BASH ?
NOPE! SPENDING A QUIET EVENING AT HOME!

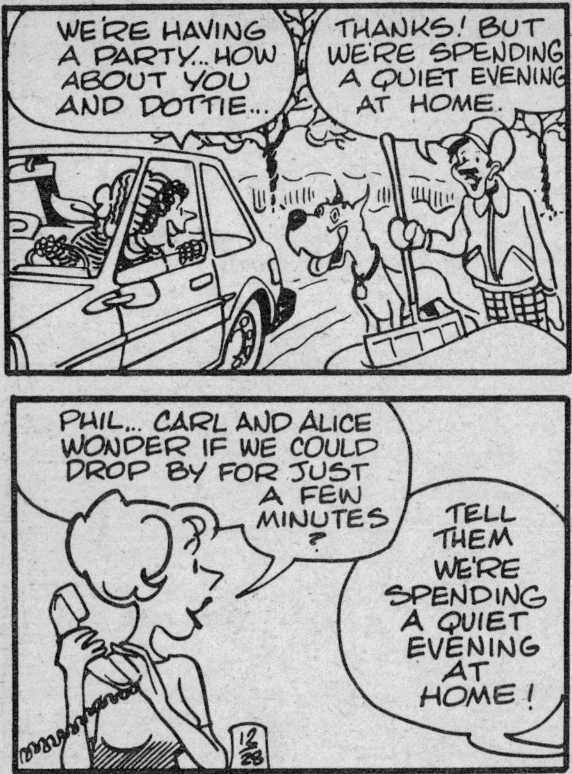
WE'RE HAVING A PARTY...HOW ABOUT YOU AND DOTTIE...
THANKS! BUT WE'RE SPENDING A QUIET EVENING AT HOME.
PHIL... CARL AND ALICE WONDER IF WE COULD DROP BY FOR JUST A FEW MINUTES ?
TELL THEM WE'RE SPENDING A QUIET EVENING AT HOME !

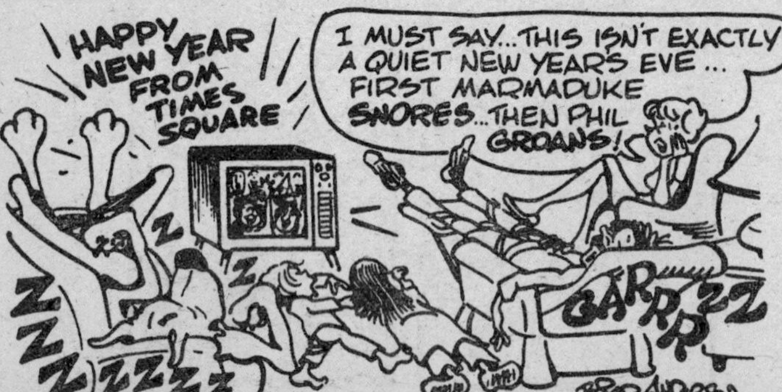
HAPPY NEW YEAR FROM TIMES SQUARE
I MUST SAY...THIS ISN'T EXACTLY A QUIET NEW YEAR'S EVE ... FIRST MARMADUKE SNORES...THEN PHIL GROANS!
ZZZ
NNNZZZZZ
GARRR ZZZ
BRAD ANDERSON

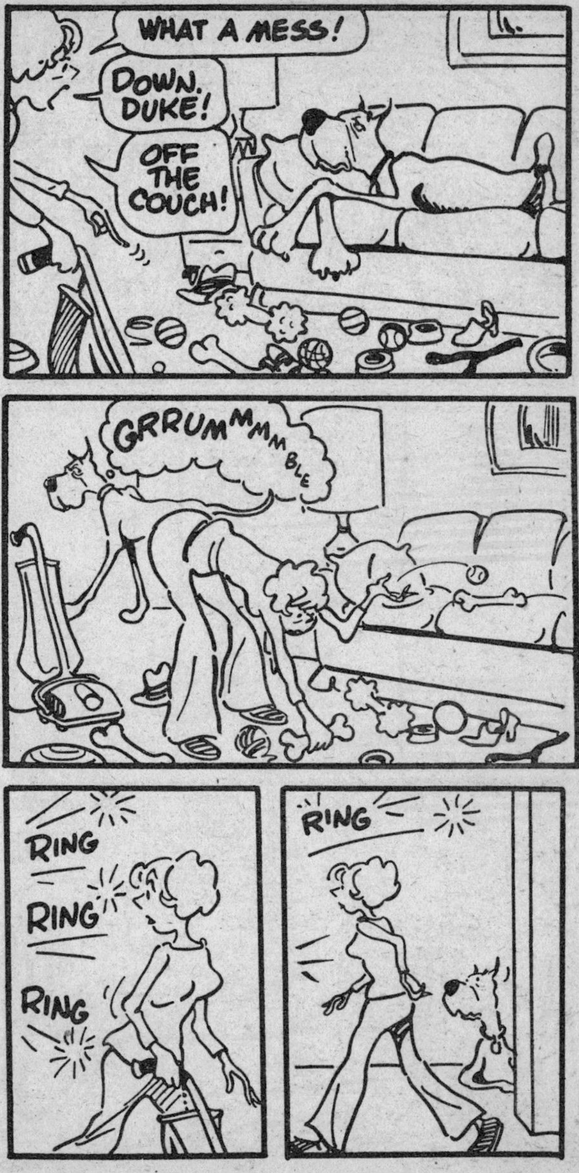
WHAT A MESS!
DOWN, DUKE!
OFF THE COUCH!
GRRUMMMMMBLE
RING
RING
RING
RING

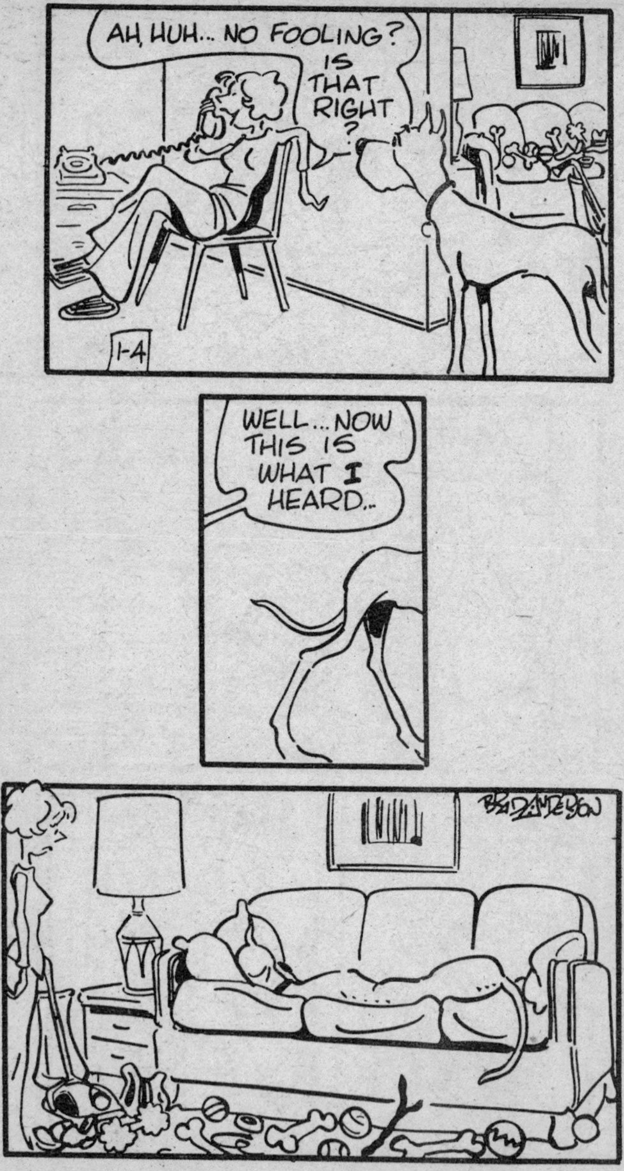
AH, HUH... NO FOOLING?
IS THAT RIGHT ?
1-4
WELL... NOW THIS IS WHAT I HEARD..

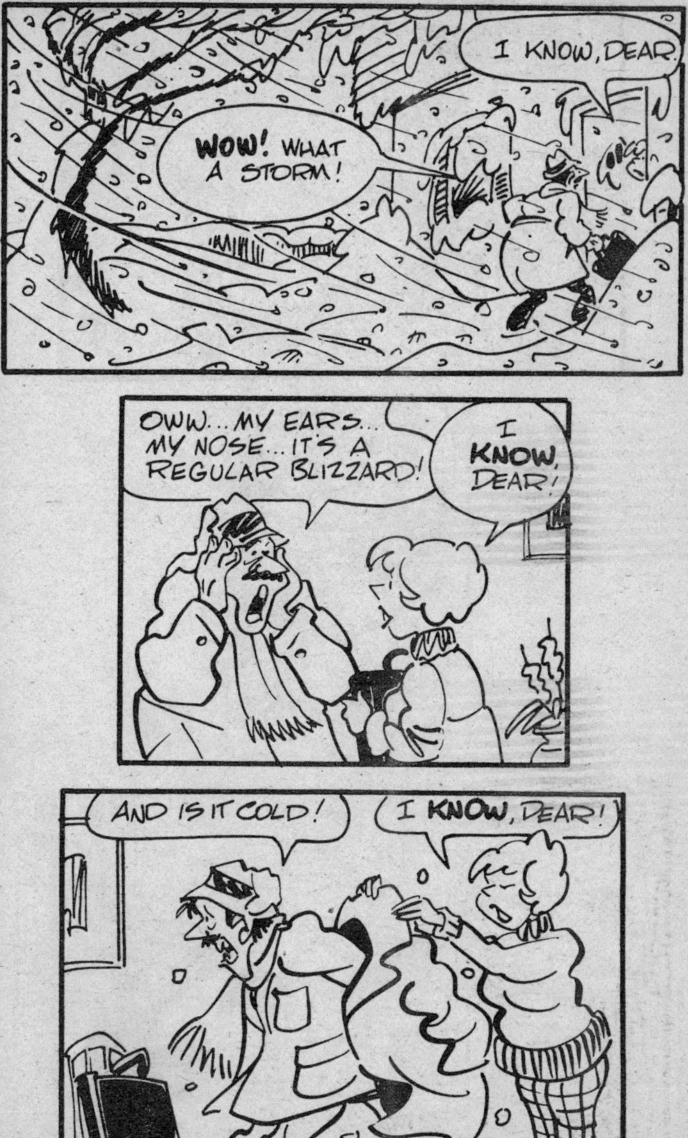
WOW! WHAT A STORM!
I KNOW, DEAR.
OWW... MY EARS... MY NOSE... IT'S A REGULAR BLIZZARD!
I KNOW, DEAR!
AND IS IT COLD!
I KNOW, DEAR!

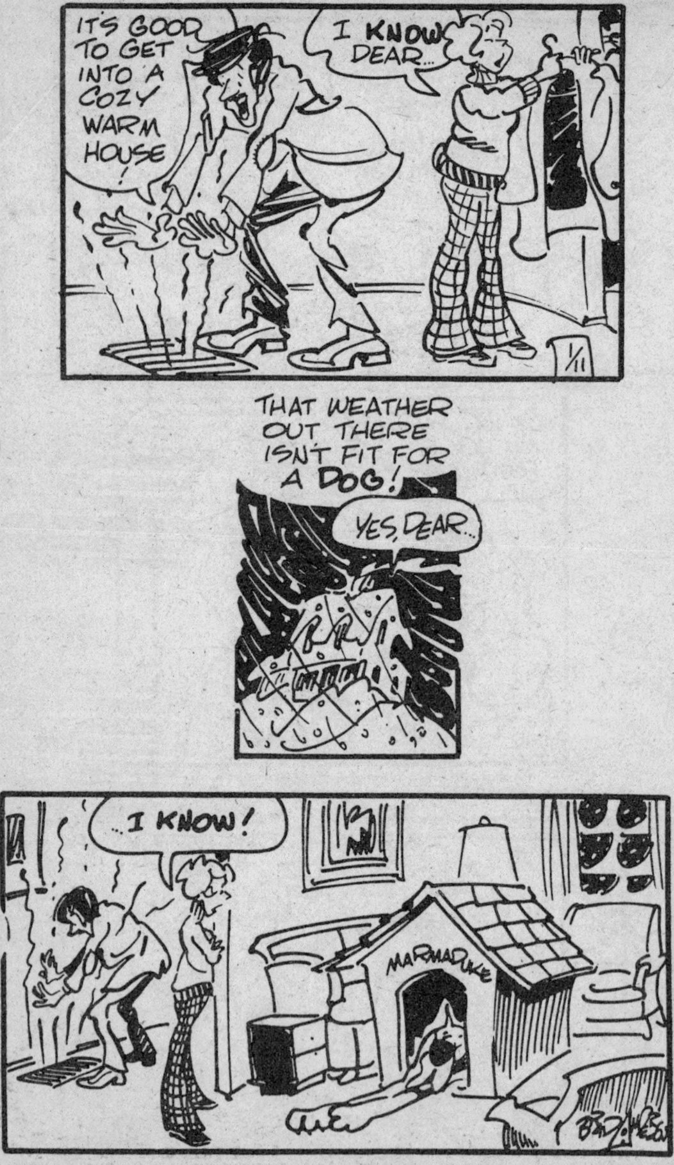
IT'S GOOD TO GET INTO A COZY WARM HOUSE!
I KNOW DEAR...
1/11
THAT WEATHER OUT THERE ISN'T FIT FOR A DOG!
YES, DEAR...
...I KNOW!
MARMADUKE

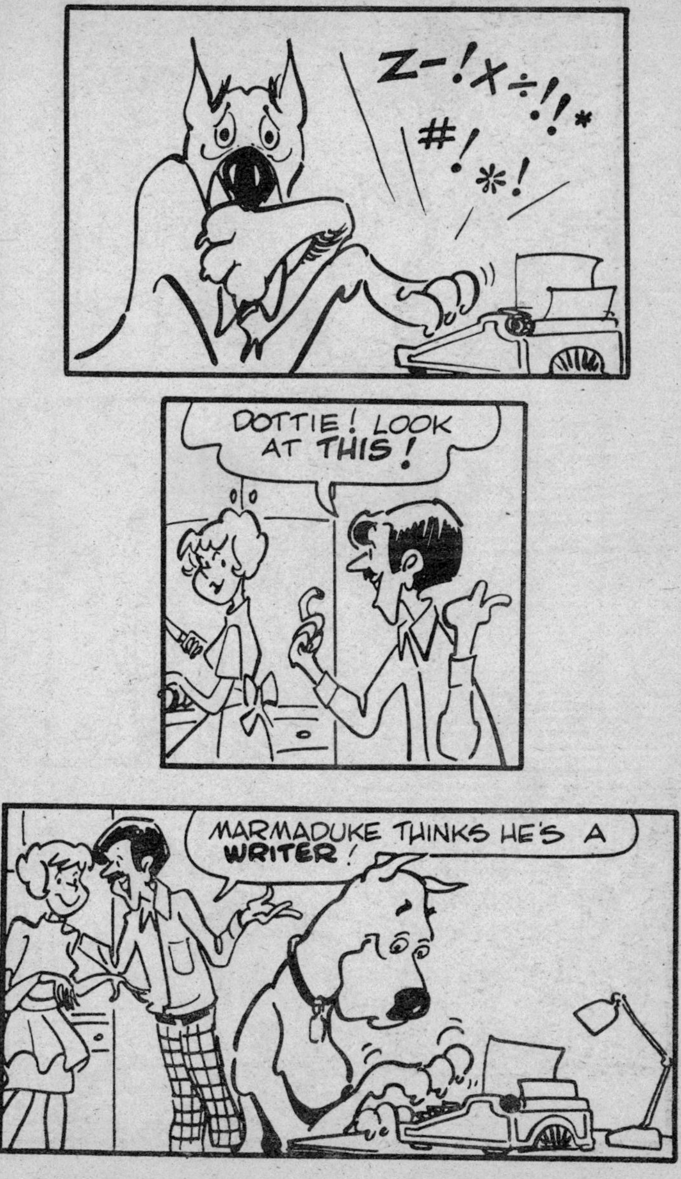
Z-!X÷!!*#!*!
DOTTIE! LOOK AT THIS!
MARMADUKE THINKS HE'S A WRITER!

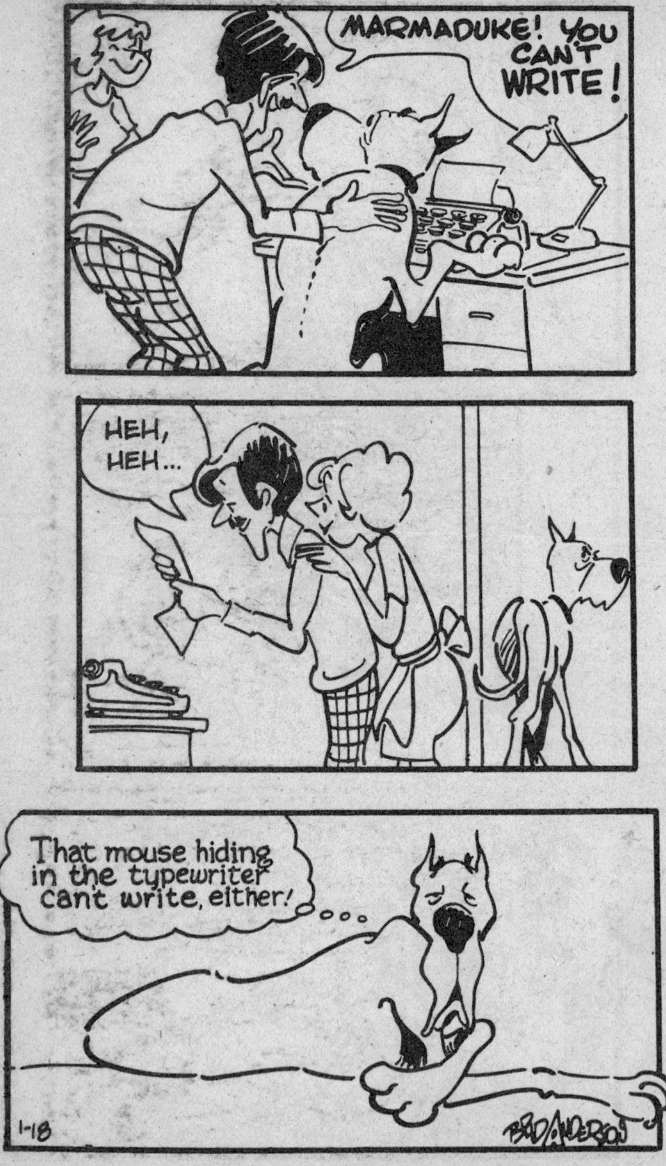
MARMADUKE! YOU CAN'T WRITE!
HEH, HEH...
That mouse hiding in the typewriter can't write, either!
1-18
BRAD ANDERSON

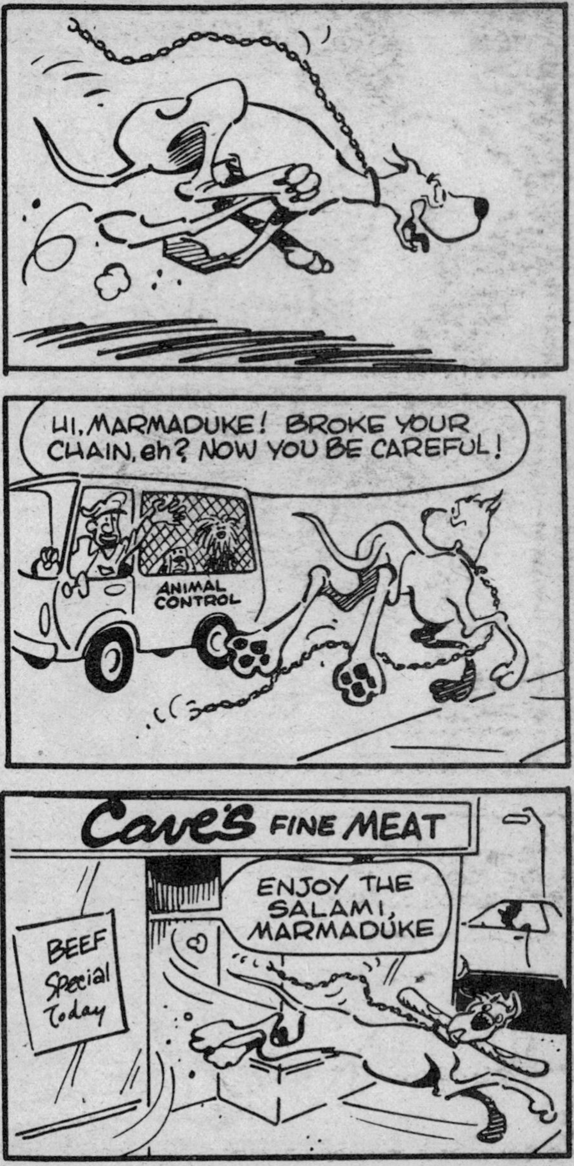
HI, MARMADUKE! BROKE YOUR CHAIN, eh? NOW YOU BE CAREFUL!
ANIMAL CONTROL
Cave's FINE MEAT
ENJOY THE SALAMI, MARMADUKE
BEEF Special Today

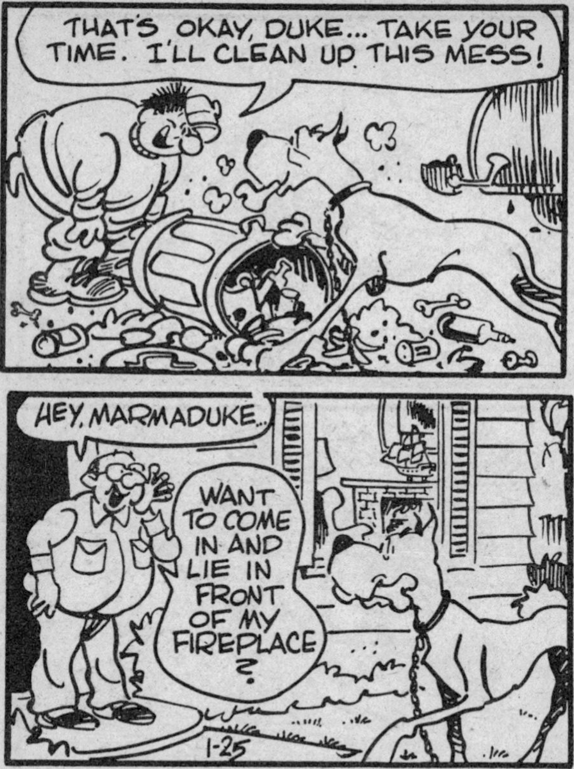
THAT'S OKAY, DUKE... TAKE YOUR TIME. I'LL CLEAN UP THIS MESS!
HEY, MARMADUKE...
WANT TO COME IN AND LIE IN FRONT OF MY FIREPLACE?
1-25

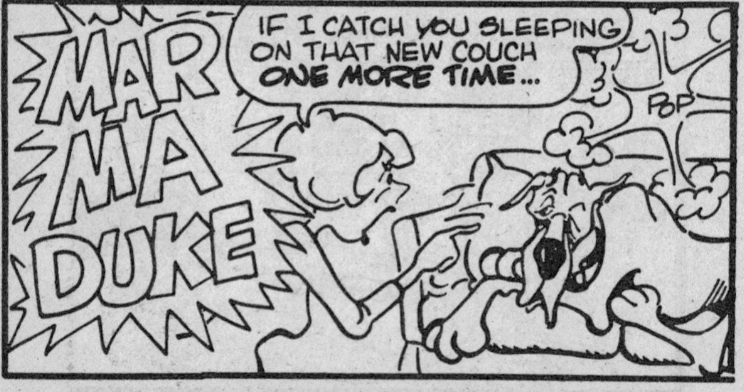
MARMADUKE
IF I CATCH YOU SLEEPING ON THAT NEW COUCH **ONE MORE TIME...**
POP

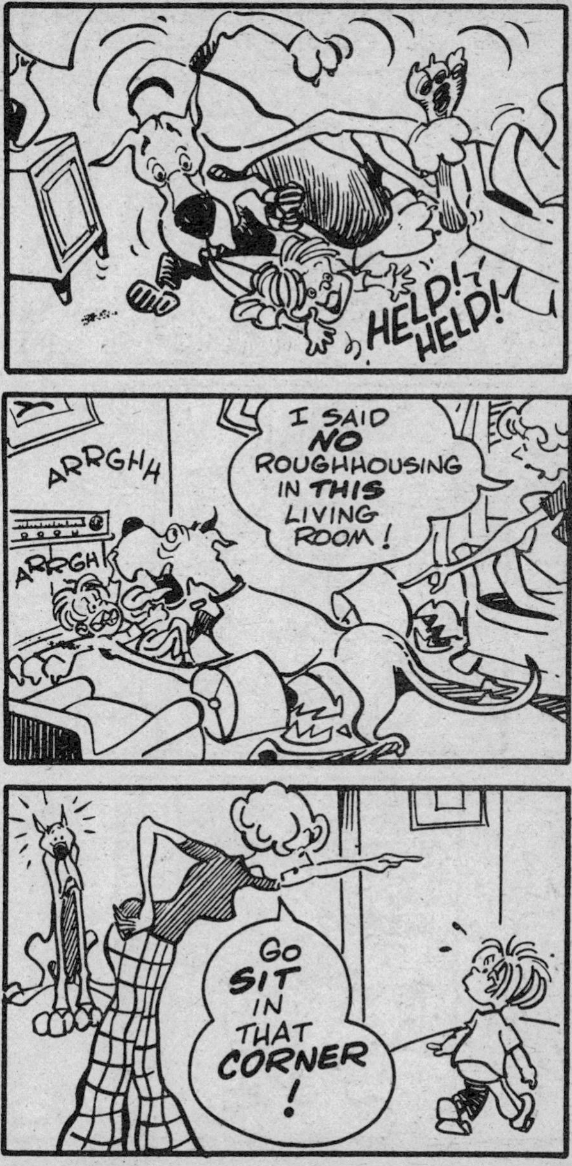
HELP! HELP!
ARRGHH
ARRGH
I SAID NO ROUGHHOUSING IN THIS LIVING ROOM!
GO SIT IN THAT CORNER!

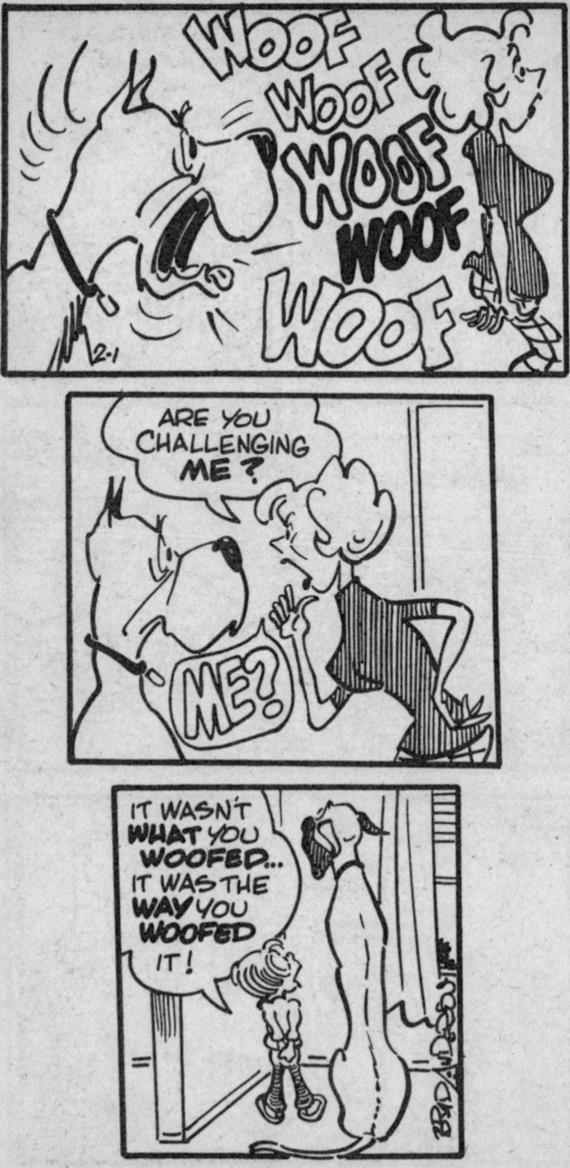
WOOF WOOF WOOF WOOF WOOF
2-1
ARE YOU CHALLENGING ME?
ME?
IT WASN'T WHAT YOU WOOFED... IT WAS THE WAY YOU WOOFED IT!

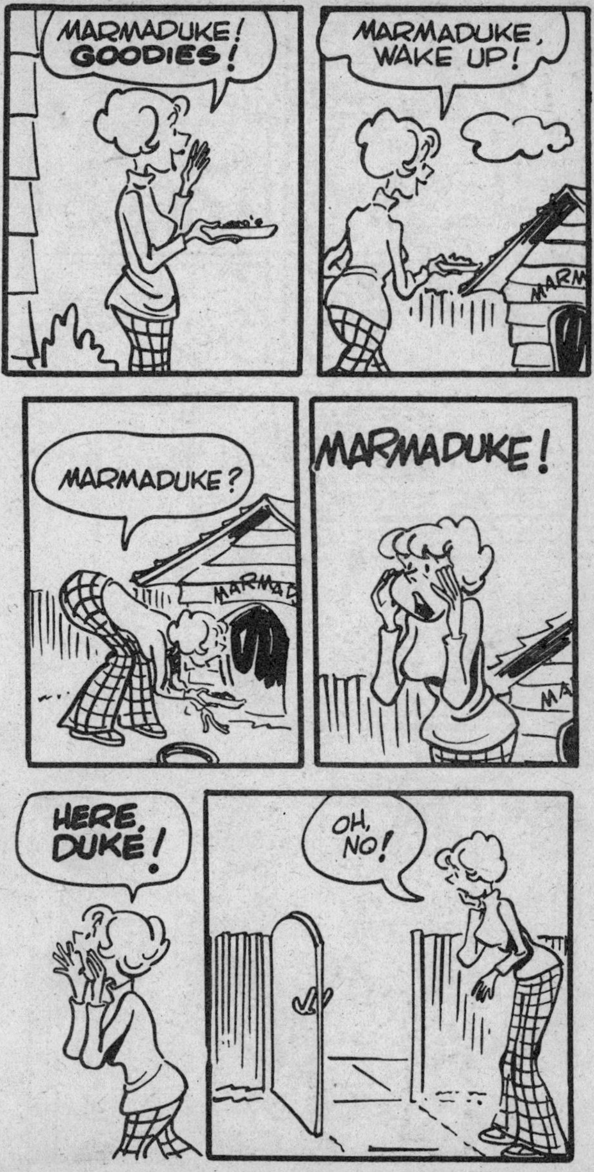
MARMADUKE! GOODIES!
MARMADUKE, WAKE UP!
MARM
MARMADUKE?
MARMAD
MARMADUKE!
MA
HERE, DUKE!
OH, NO!

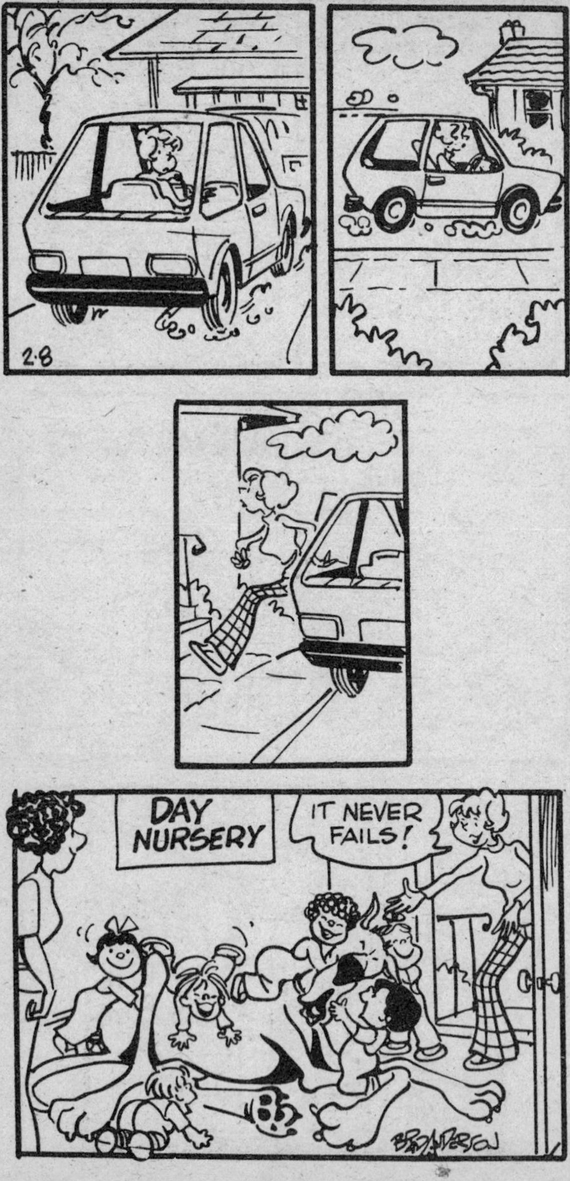
2·8
DAY NURSERY
IT NEVER FAILS!
BRAD ANDERSON

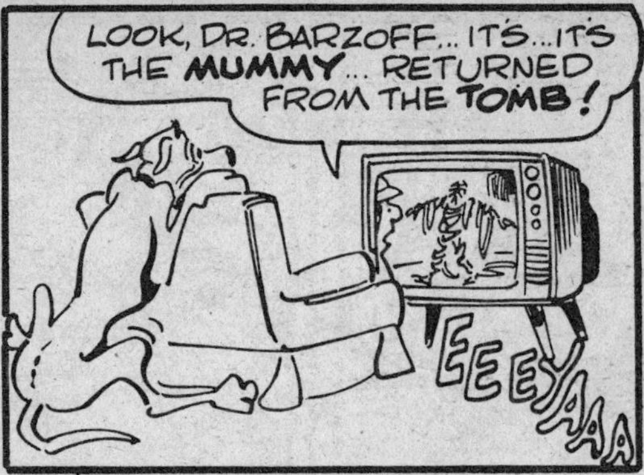
LOOK, DR. BARZOFF... IT'S...IT'S THE **MUMMY**... RETURNED FROM THE **TOMB**!
EEEYAAAA

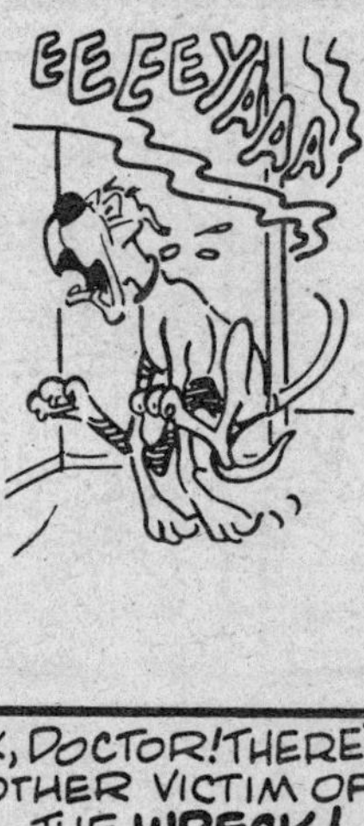
EEEEYAAAA

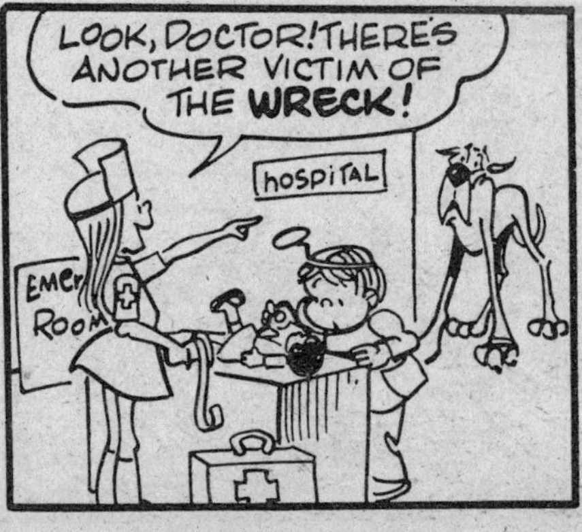
LOOK, DOCTOR! THERE'S ANOTHER VICTIM OF THE **WRECK**!
hospital
EMER ROOM

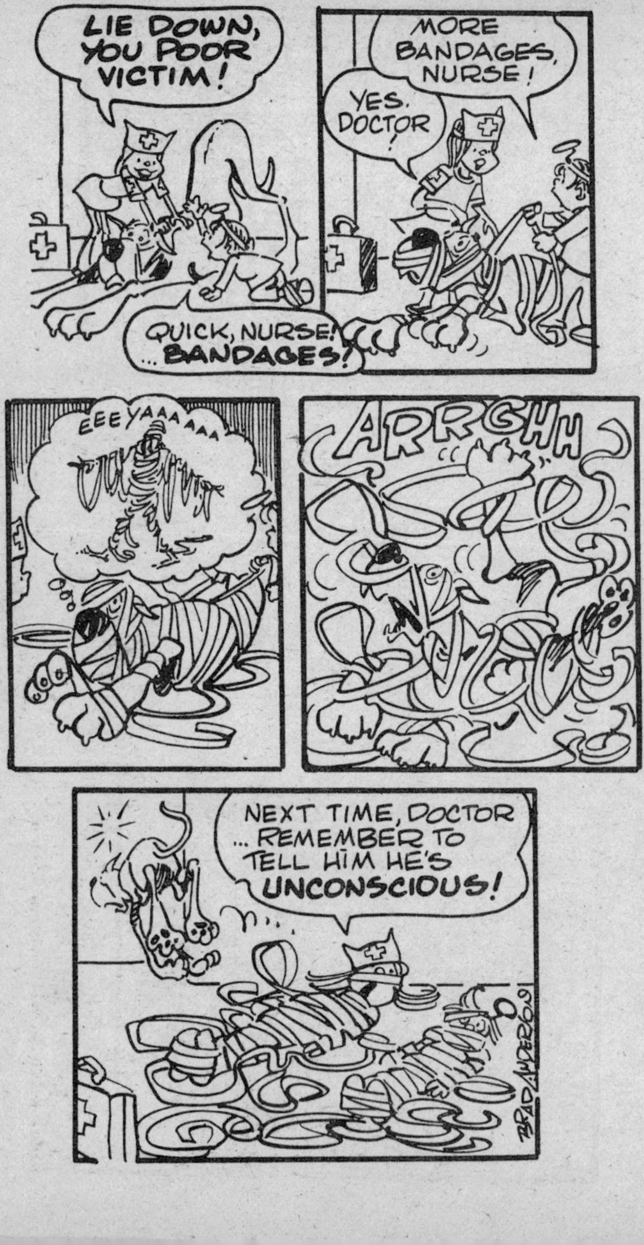
LIE DOWN, YOU POOR VICTIM!
QUICK, NURSE! ... BANDAGES!
MORE BANDAGES, NURSE!
YES, DOCTOR!
EEEYAAAAAA
ARRGHH
NEXT TIME, DOCTOR ... REMEMBER TO TELL HIM HE'S UNCONSCIOUS!
BRAD ANDERSON

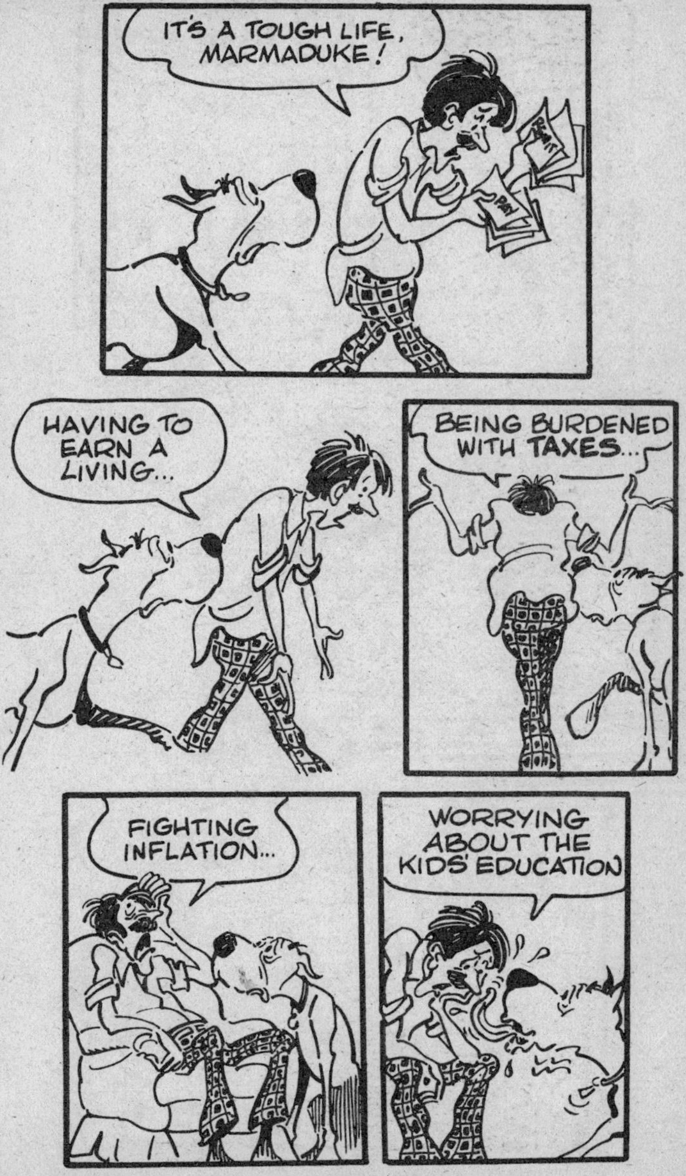
IT'S A TOUGH LIFE, MARMADUKE!
PAY
HAVING TO EARN A LIVING...
BEING BURDENED WITH TAXES...
FIGHTING INFLATION...
WORRYING ABOUT THE KIDS' EDUCATION

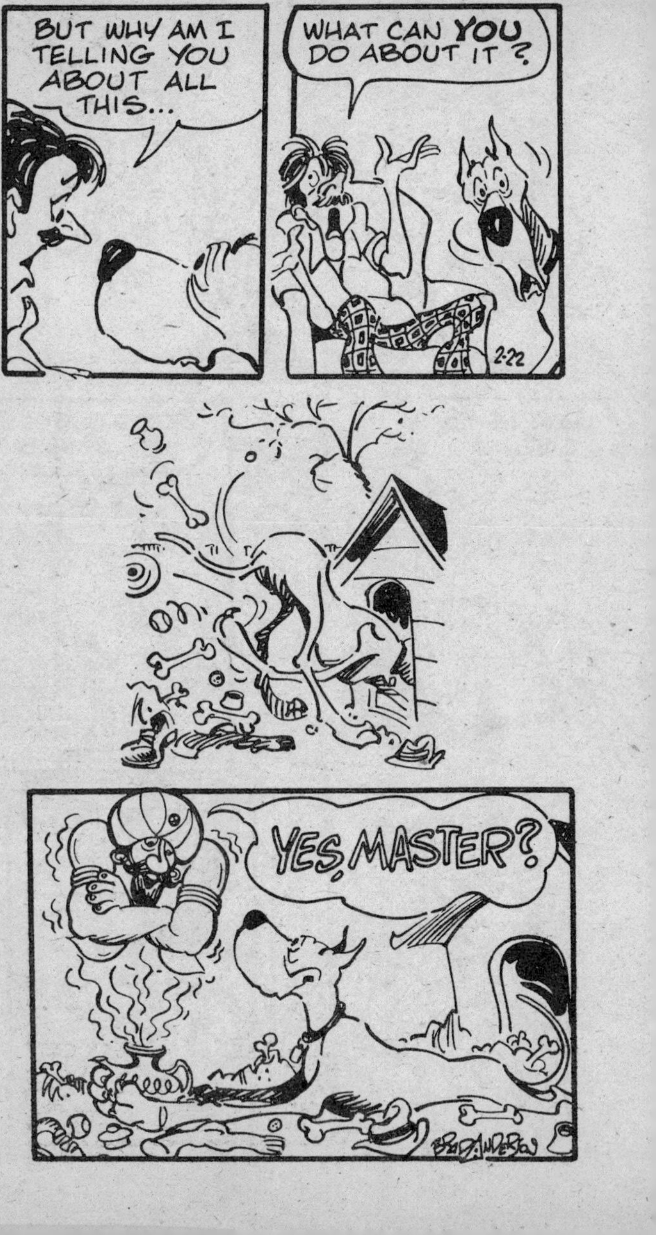
BUT WHY AM I TELLING YOU ABOUT ALL THIS...
WHAT CAN YOU DO ABOUT IT ?
2-22
YES, MASTER?
BRAD ANDERSON

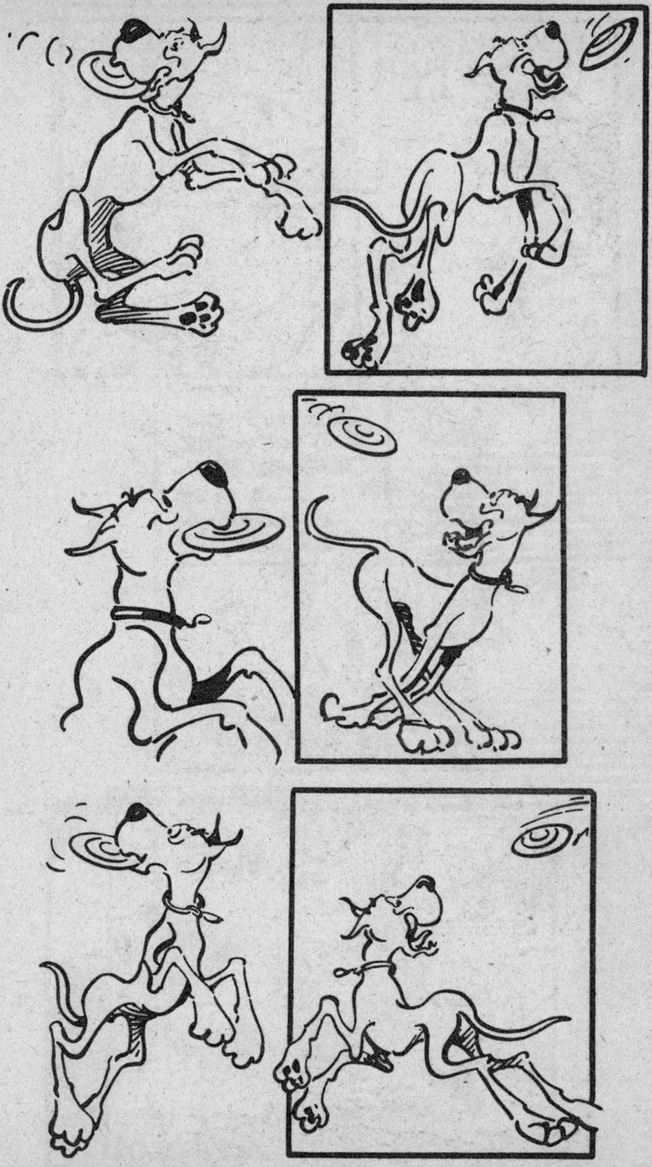

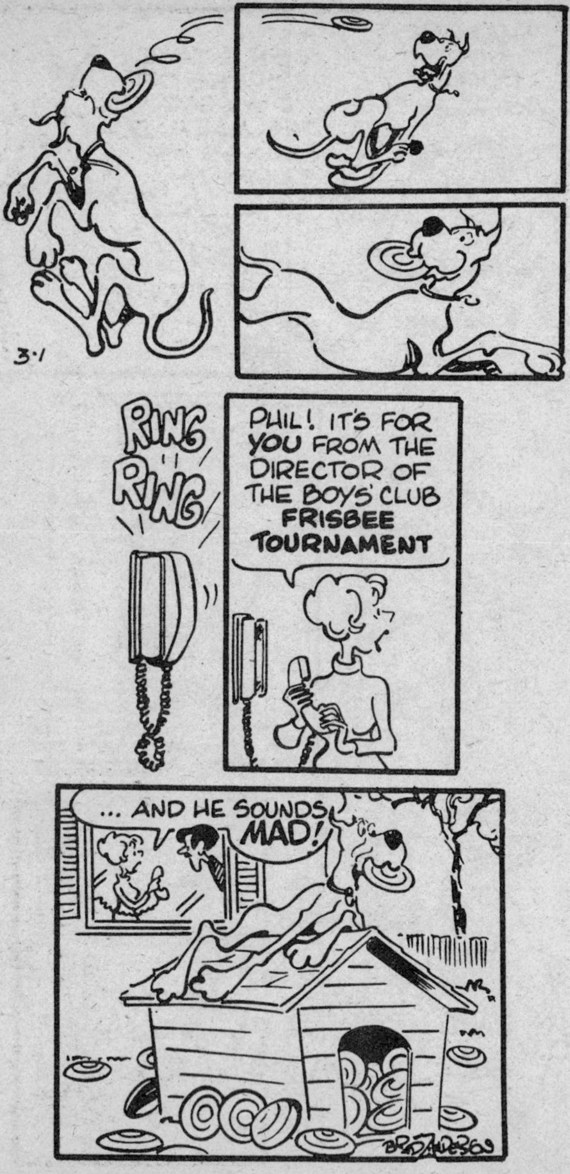
3-1
RING
RING
PHIL! IT'S FOR YOU FROM THE DIRECTOR OF THE BOYS' CLUB FRISBEE TOURNAMENT
... AND HE SOUNDS MAD!
BRAD ANDERSON

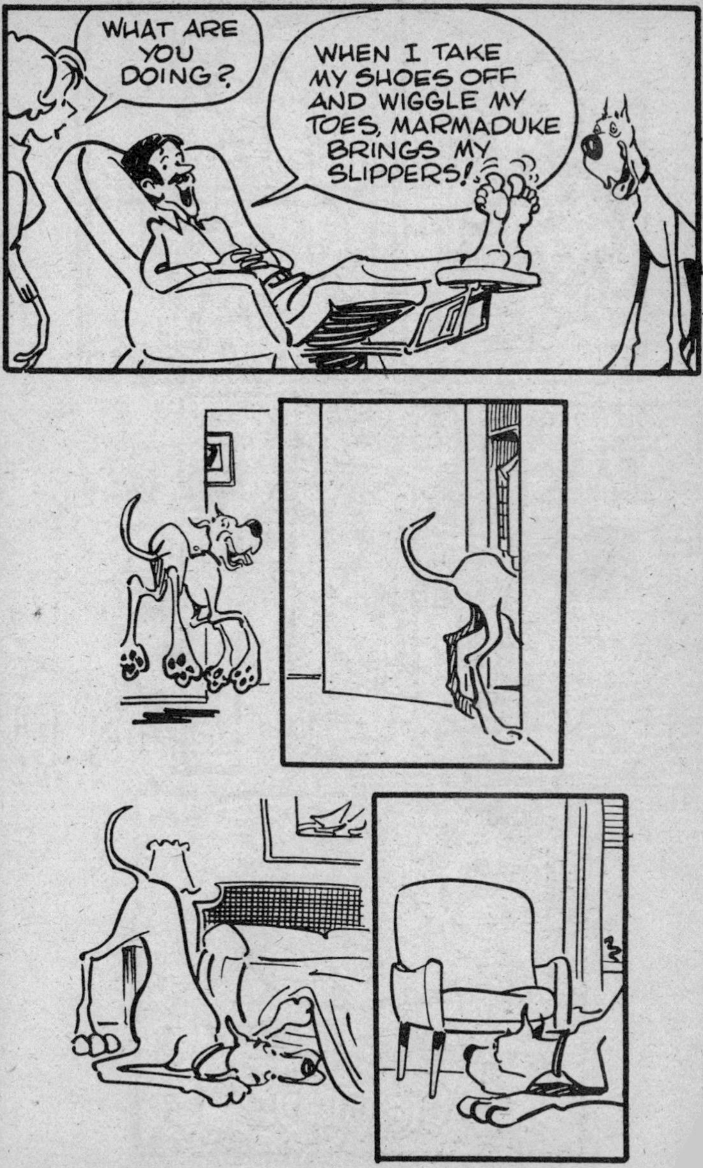
WHAT ARE YOU DOING?
WHEN I TAKE MY SHOES OFF AND WIGGLE MY TOES, MARMADUKE BRINGS MY SLIPPERS!

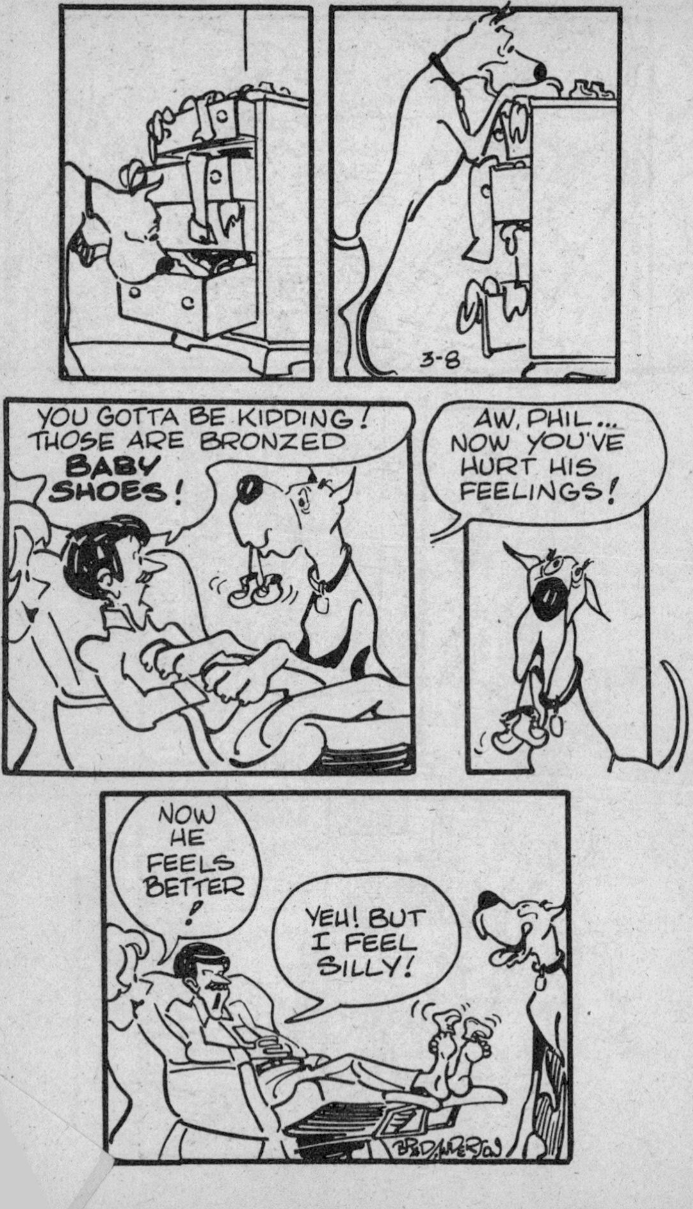
3-8
YOU GOTTA BE KIDDING! THOSE ARE BRONZED BABY SHOES!
AW, PHIL... NOW YOU'VE HURT HIS FEELINGS!
NOW HE FEELS BETTER!
YEH! BUT I FEEL SILLY!
BRAD ANDERSON

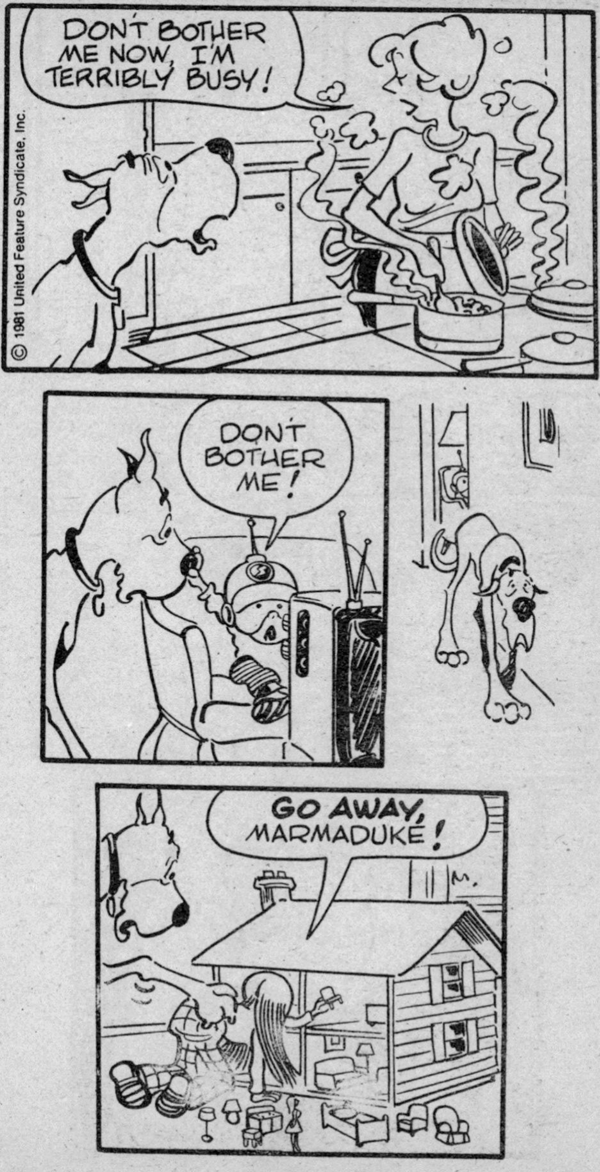
DON'T BOTHER ME NOW, I'M TERRIBLY BUSY!
DON'T BOTHER ME!
GO AWAY, MARMADUKE!

WHAT'S THE MATTER, DUKE?
SUNDAY
NEED A LITTLE SCRATCH BEHIND THE EAR?
3·15
JUST GIVE HIM A LITTLE BIT OF LOVING AND YOU GET A **WHOLE** LOT BACK!

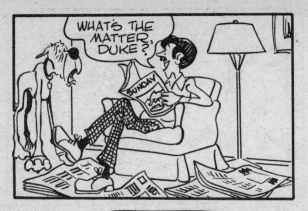

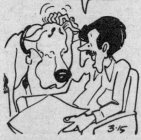

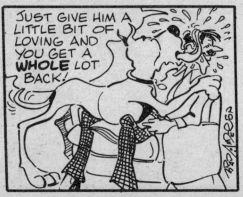

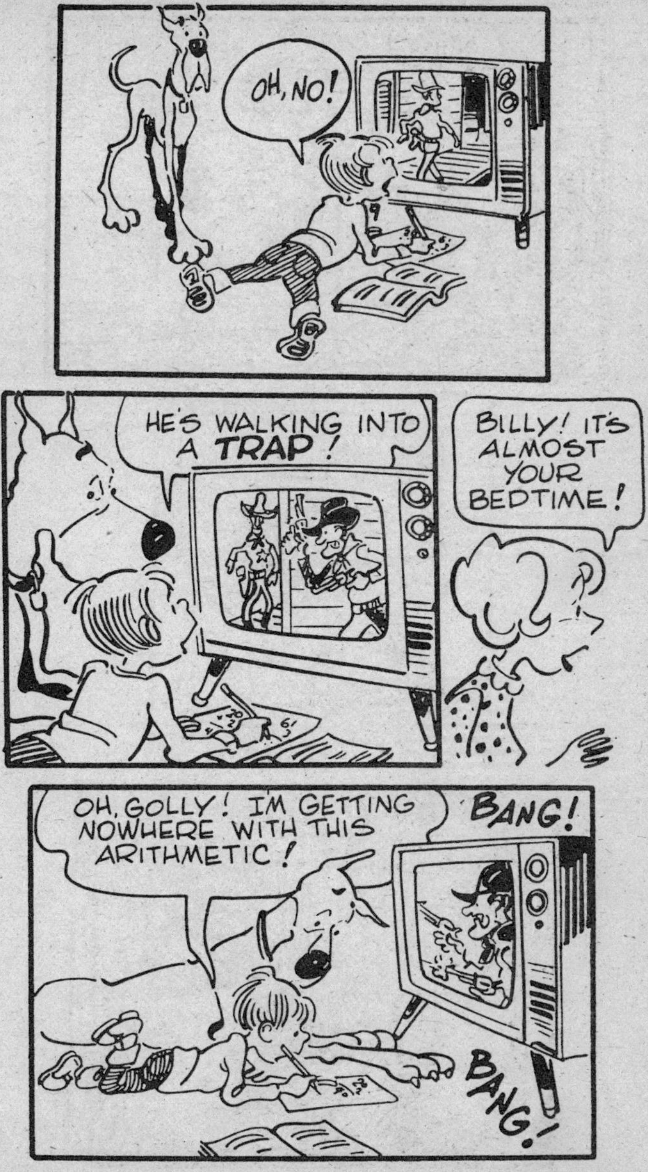
OH, NO!
HE'S WALKING INTO A **TRAP**!
BILLY! IT'S ALMOST YOUR BEDTIME!
OH, GOLLY! I'M GETTING NOWHERE WITH THIS ARITHMETIC!
BANG!
BANG!

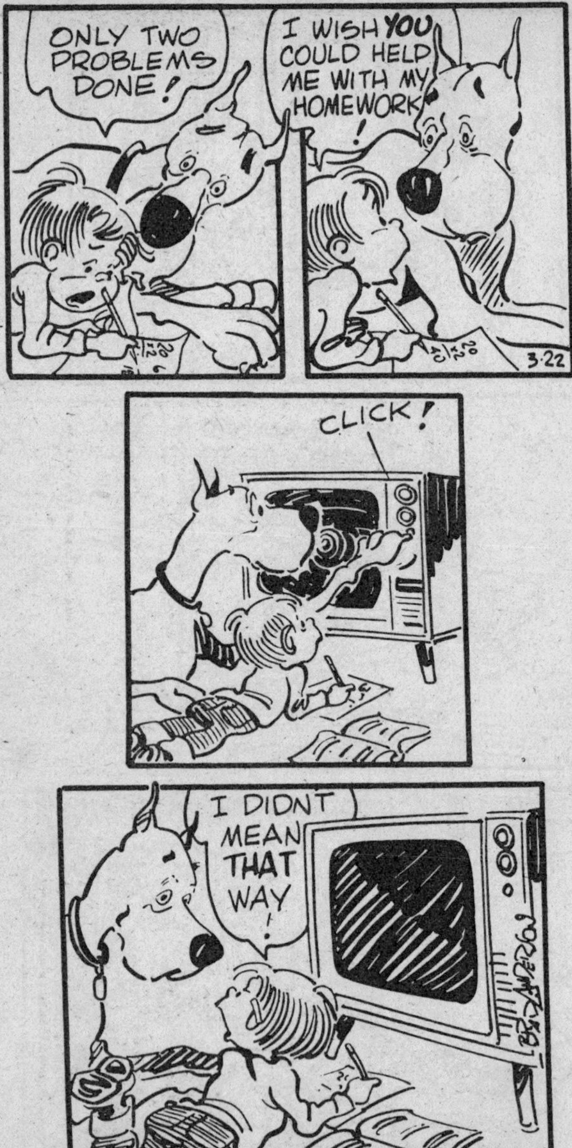
ONLY TWO PROBLEMS DONE!
I WISH YOU COULD HELP ME WITH MY HOMEWORK!
3·22
CLICK!
I DIDNT MEAN THAT WAY!

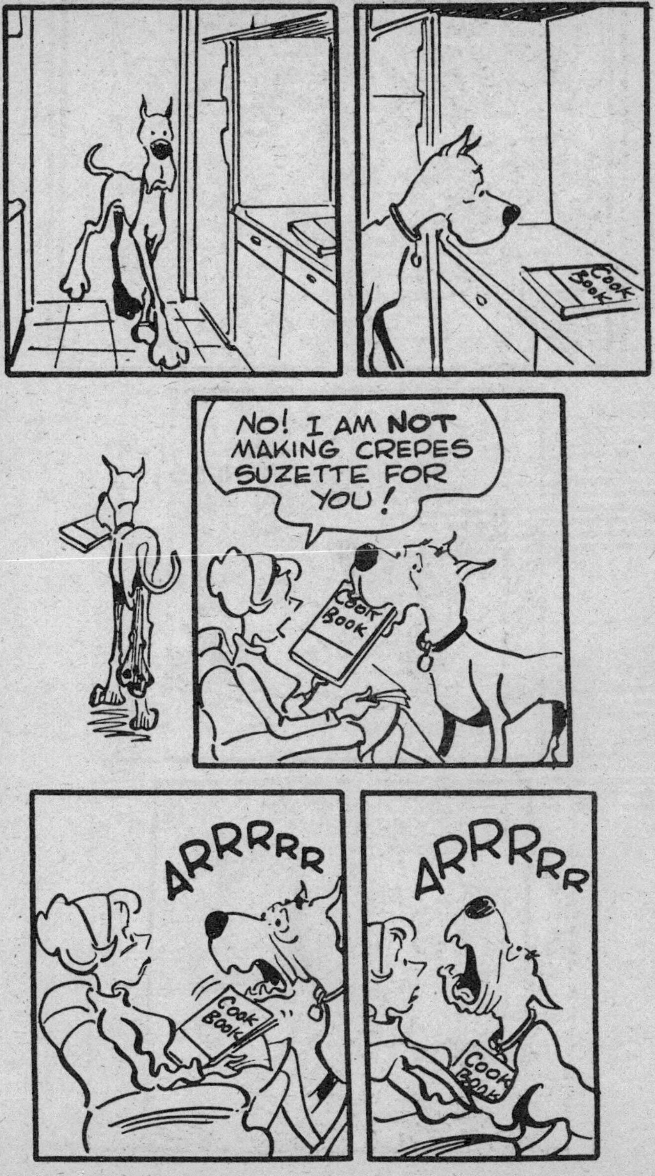

Cook Book
NO! I AM NOT MAKING CREPES SUZETTE FOR YOU!
Cook Book
ARRRRRR
Cook Book
ARRRRRR
Cook Book

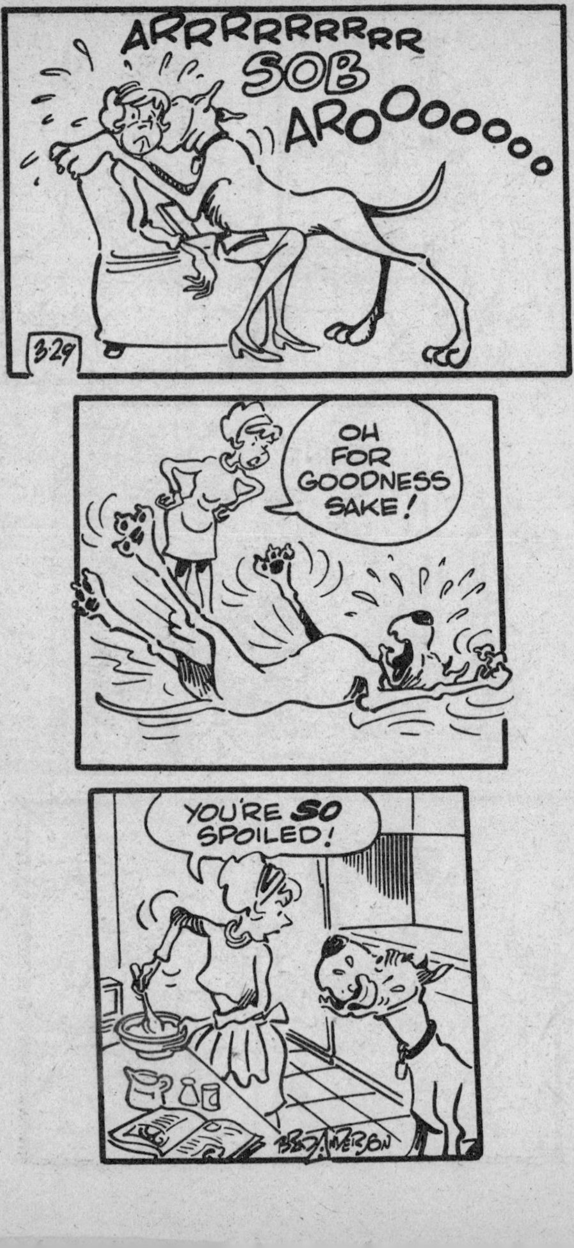
ARRRRRRRRR
SOB
AROOOOOOO
3·29
OH FOR GOODNESS SAKE!
YOU'RE SO SPOILED!

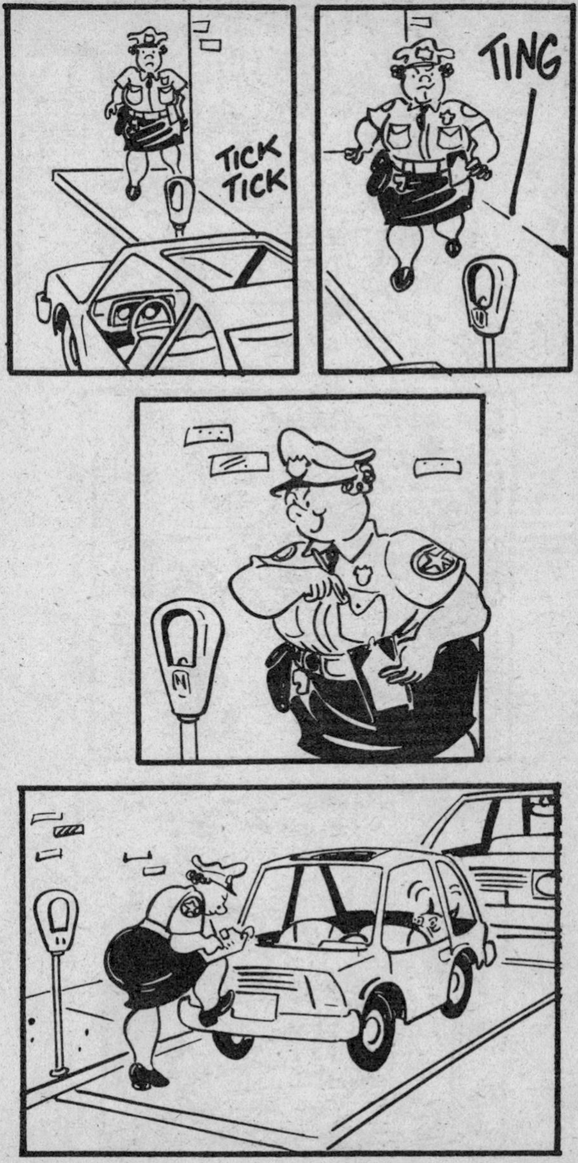
TICK
TICK
TING

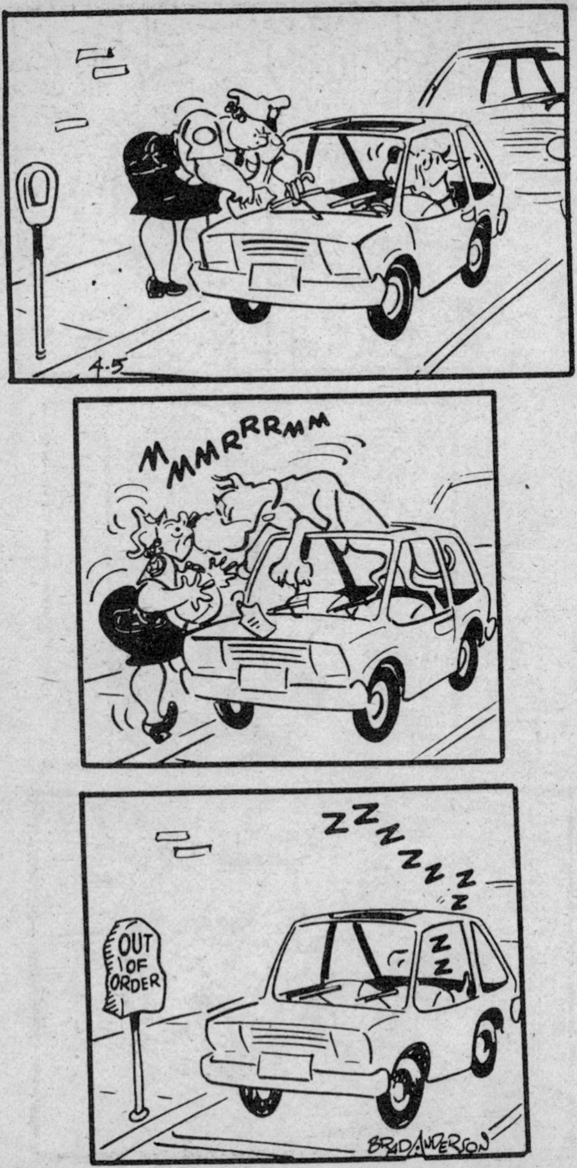
4-5
MMMRRRMM
ZZZZZZZ
ZZ
OUT OF ORDER
BRAD ANDERSON

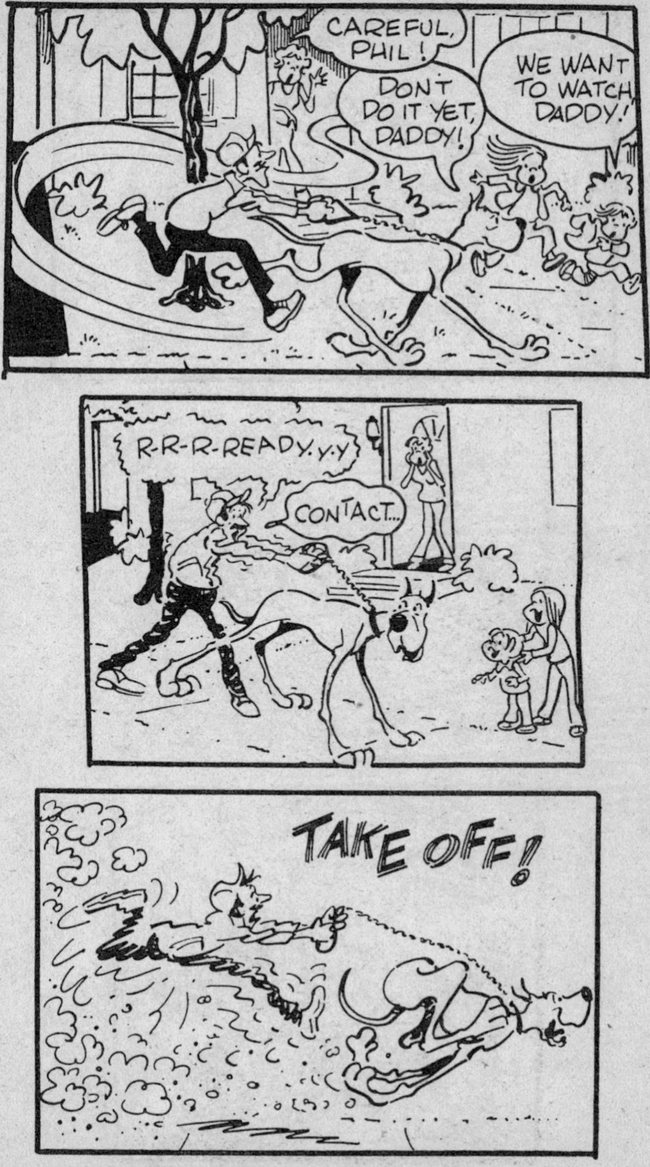
CAREFUL, PHIL!
DON'T DO IT YET, DADDY!
WE WANT TO WATCH DADDY!
R-R-R-READY-Y-Y
CONTACT...
TAKE OFF!

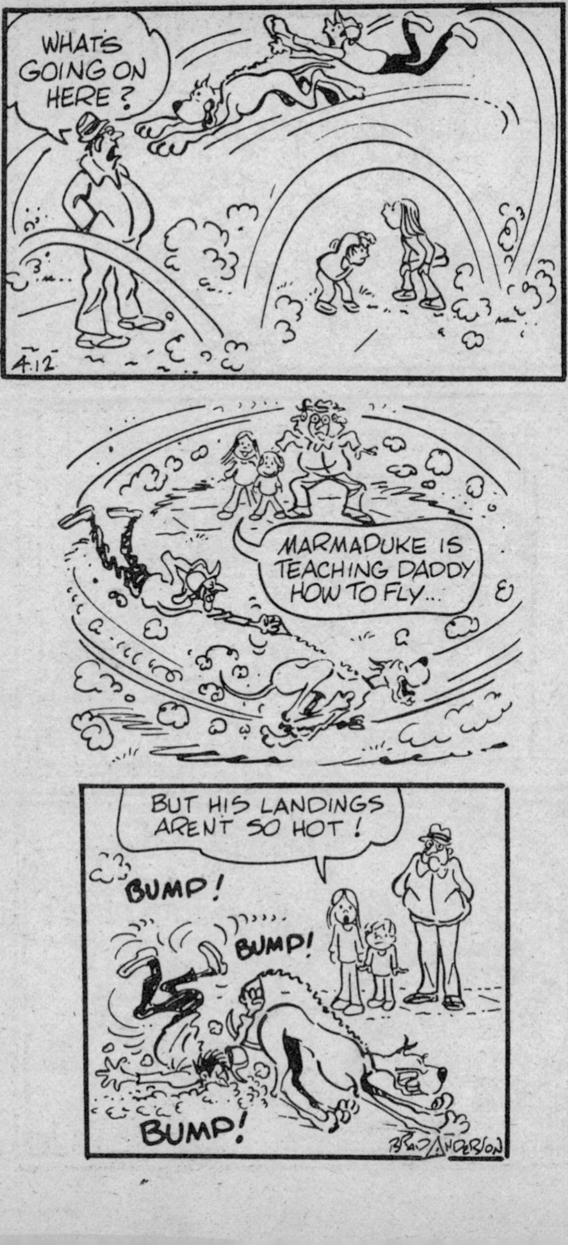
WHAT'S GOING ON HERE?
4.12
MARMADUKE IS TEACHING DADDY HOW TO FLY...
BUT HIS LANDINGS AREN'T SO HOT!
BUMP!
BUMP!
BUMP!
BRAD ANDERSON

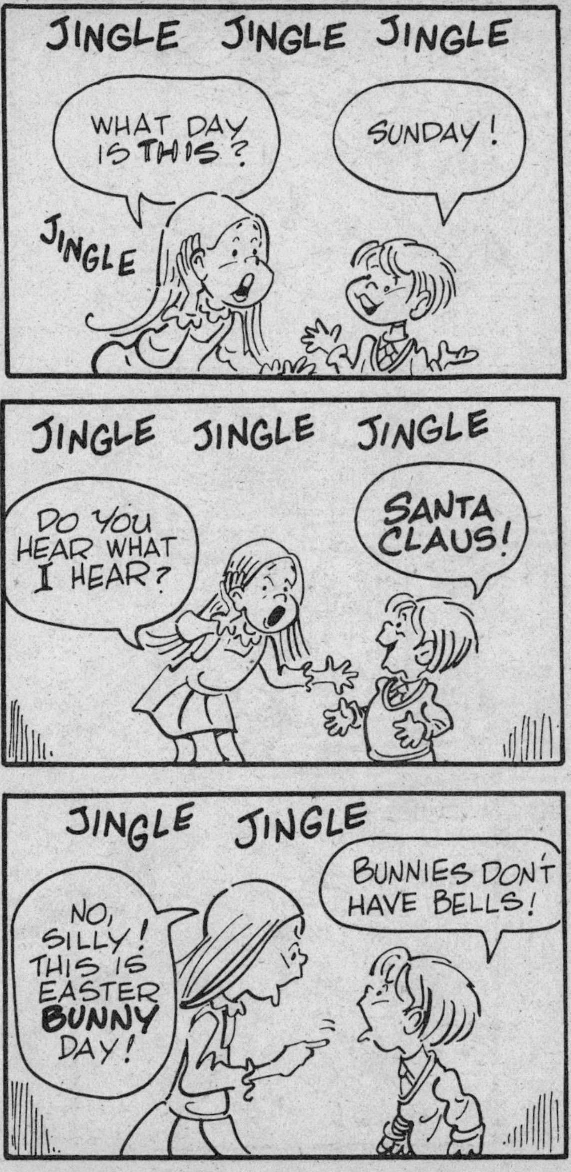
JINGLE JINGLE JINGLE
WHAT DAY IS THIS?
SUNDAY!
JINGLE
JINGLE JINGLE JINGLE
DO YOU HEAR WHAT I HEAR?
SANTA CLAUS!
JINGLE JINGLE
NO, SILLY! THIS IS EASTER BUNNY DAY!
BUNNIES DON'T HAVE BELLS!

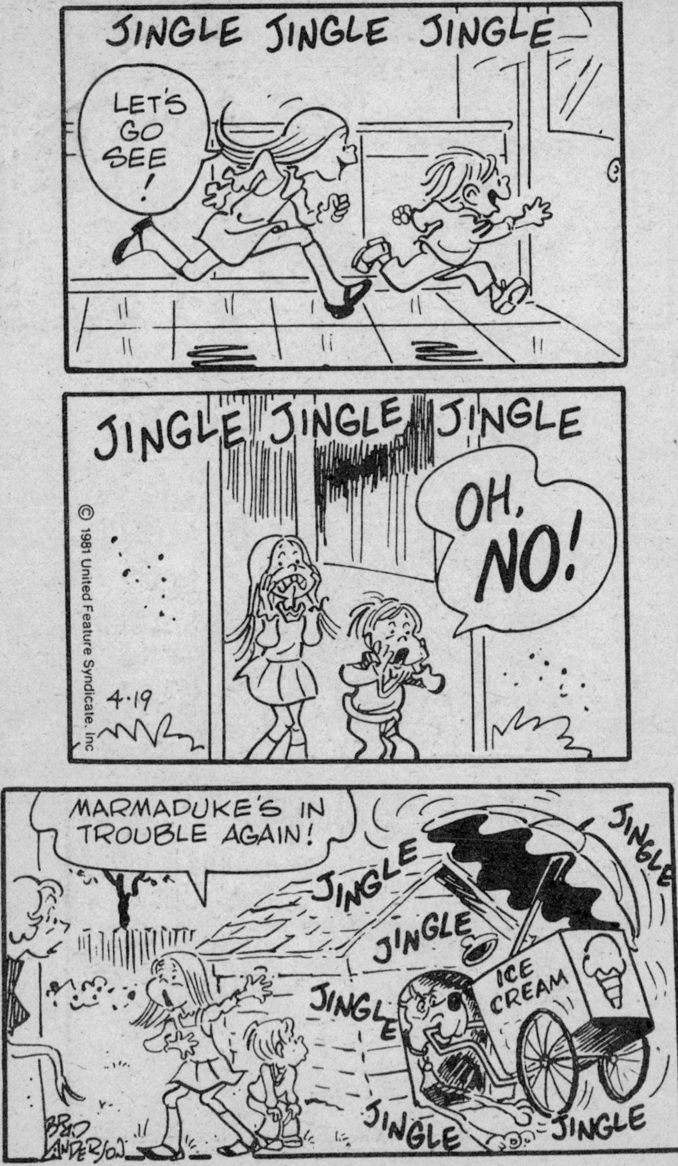
JINGLE JINGLE JINGLE
LET'S GO SEE!
JINGLE JINGLE JINGLE
OH, NO!
4·19
MARMADUKE'S IN TROUBLE AGAIN!
JINGLE
JINGLE
JINGLE
JINGLE
ICE CREAM
JINGLE
JINGLE
BRAD ANDERSON

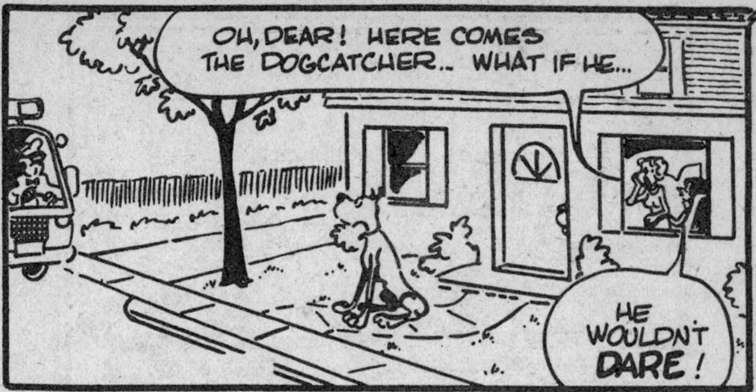
OH, DEAR! HERE COMES THE DOGCATCHER.. WHAT IF HE...
HE WOULDN'T **DARE**!

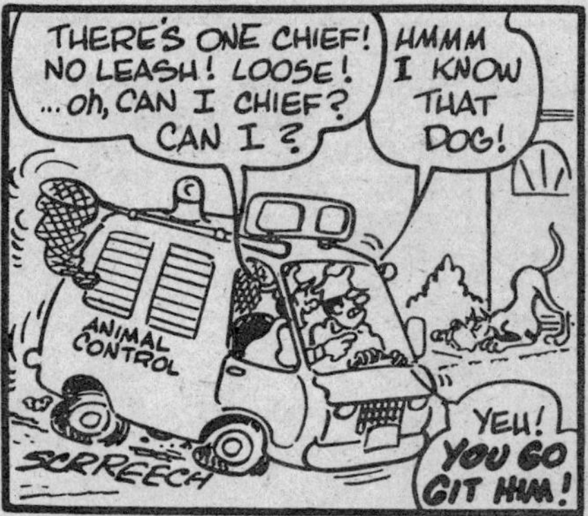
THERE'S ONE CHIEF! NO LEASH! LOOSE! ...oh, CAN I CHIEF? CAN I?
HMMM I KNOW THAT DOG!
ANIMAL CONTROL
SCRREECH
YEH! **YOU GO GIT HIM!**

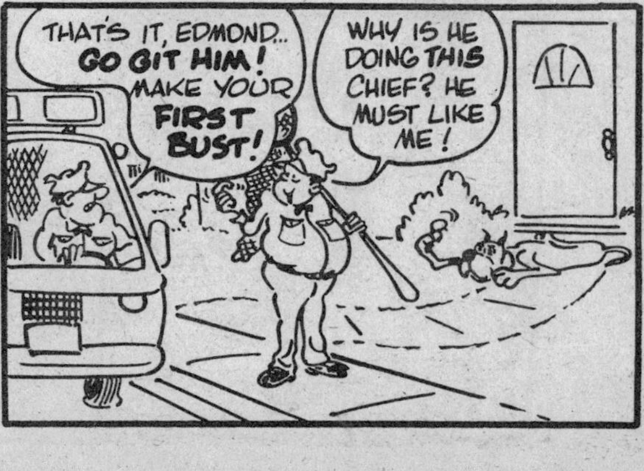
THAT'S IT, EDMOND... **GO GIT HIM!** MAKE YOUR **FIRST BUST!**
WHY IS HE DOING THIS CHIEF? HE MUST LIKE ME!

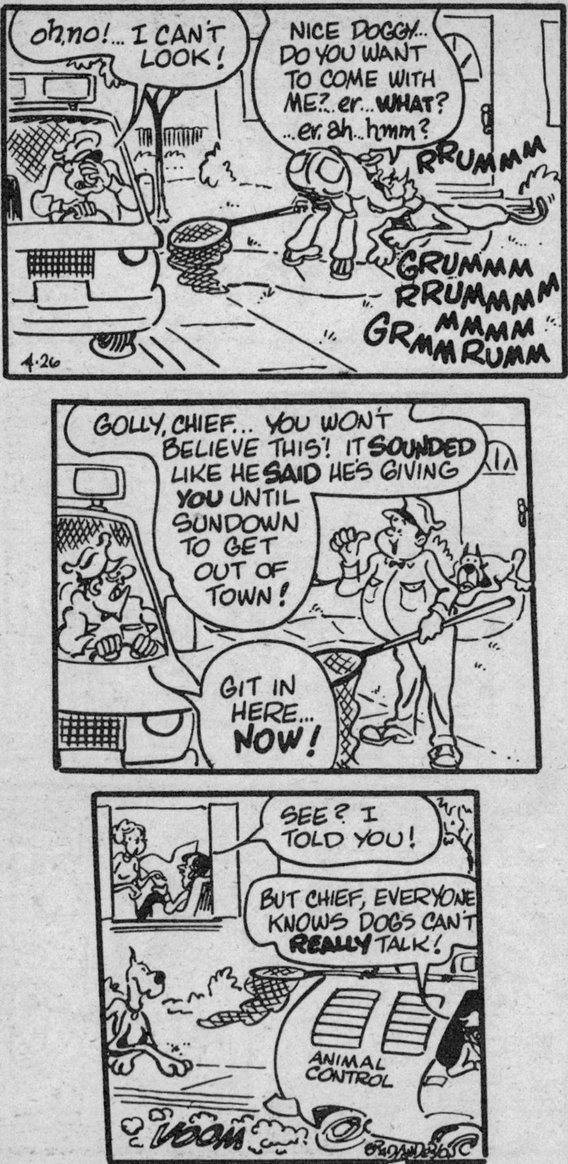
oh,no!... I CAN'T LOOK!
NICE DOGGY... DO YOU WANT TO COME WITH ME?.. er... WHAT? ...er, ah.. hmm?
RRUMMM
GRUMMM RRUMMMMM GRMMMMMRUMM
4·26
GOLLY, CHIEF... YOU WON'T BELIEVE THIS! IT SOUNDED LIKE HE SAID HE'S GIVING YOU UNTIL SUNDOWN TO GET OUT OF TOWN!
GIT IN HERE... NOW!
SEE? I TOLD YOU!
BUT CHIEF, EVERYONE KNOWS DOGS CAN'T REALLY TALK!
ANIMAL CONTROL
VOOM

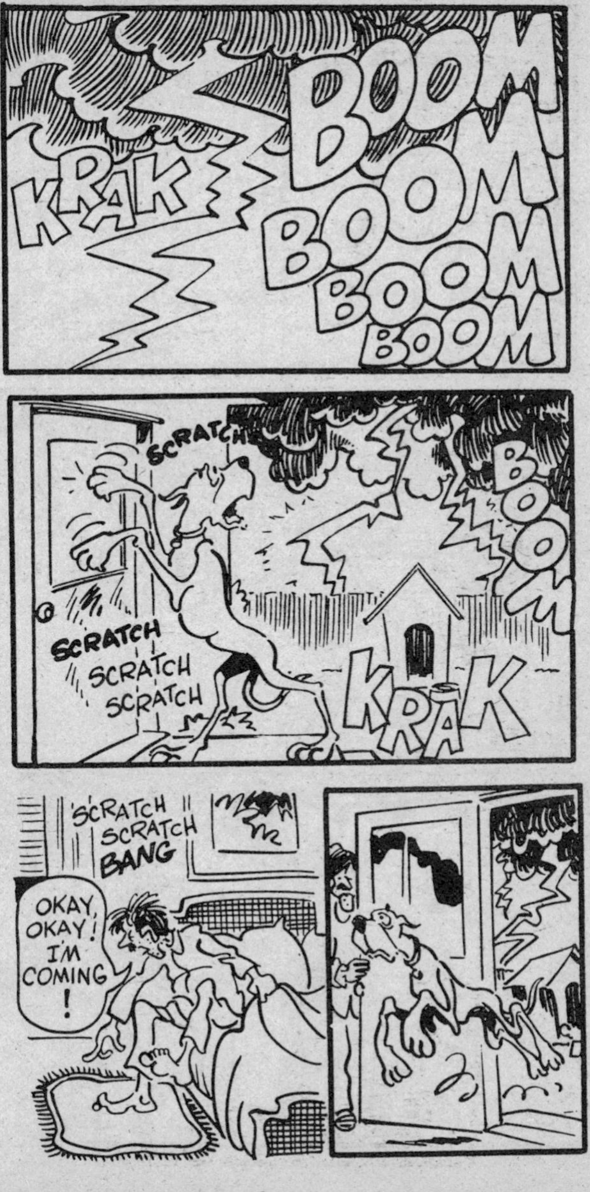
KRAK
BOOM
BOOM
BOOM
BOOM
SCRATCH
BOOM
SCRATCH
SCRATCH
SCRATCH
KRAK
SCRATCH
SCRATCH
BANG
OKAY, OKAY! I'M COMING!

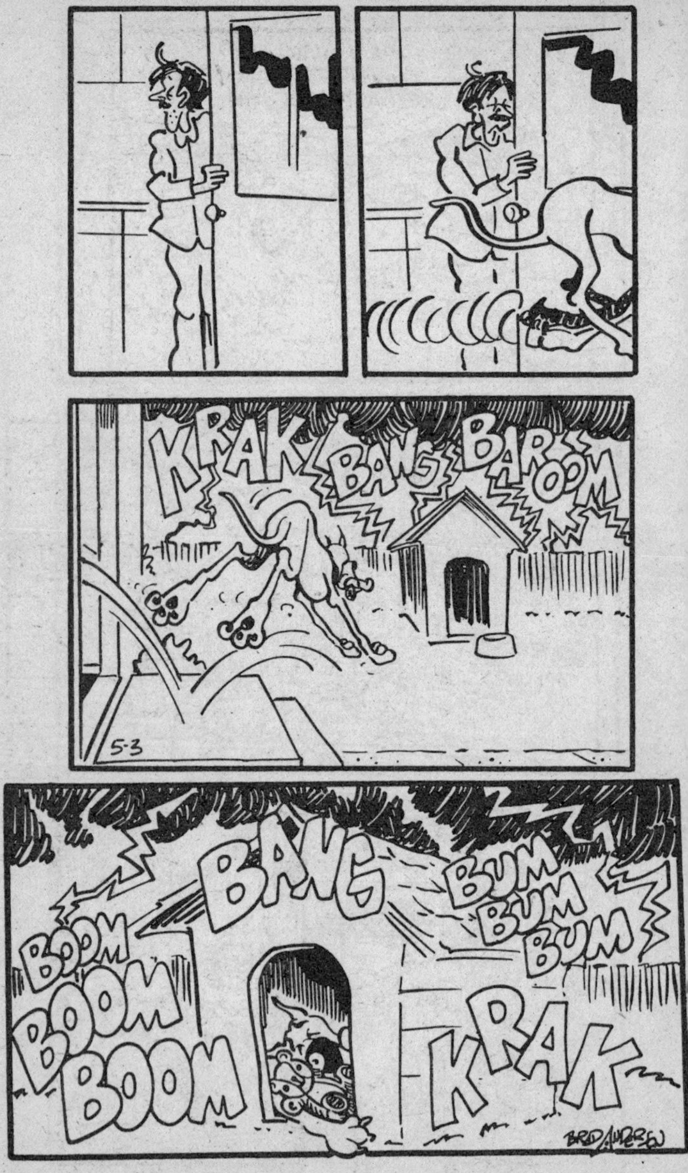
KRAK
BANG
BAROOM
5-3
BOOM
BOOM
BOOM
BANG
BUM
BUM
BUM
KRAK
BRAD ANDERSON

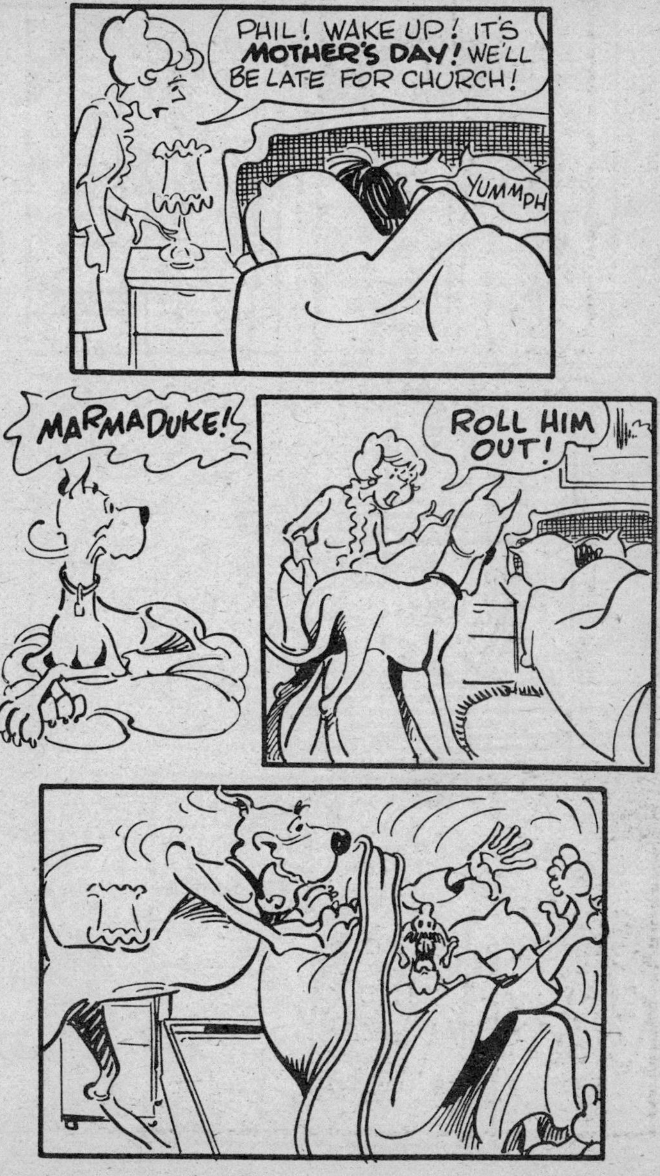
PHIL! WAKE UP! IT'S **MOTHER'S DAY!** WE'LL BE LATE FOR CHURCH!
YUMMPH
MARMADUKE!
ROLL HIM OUT!

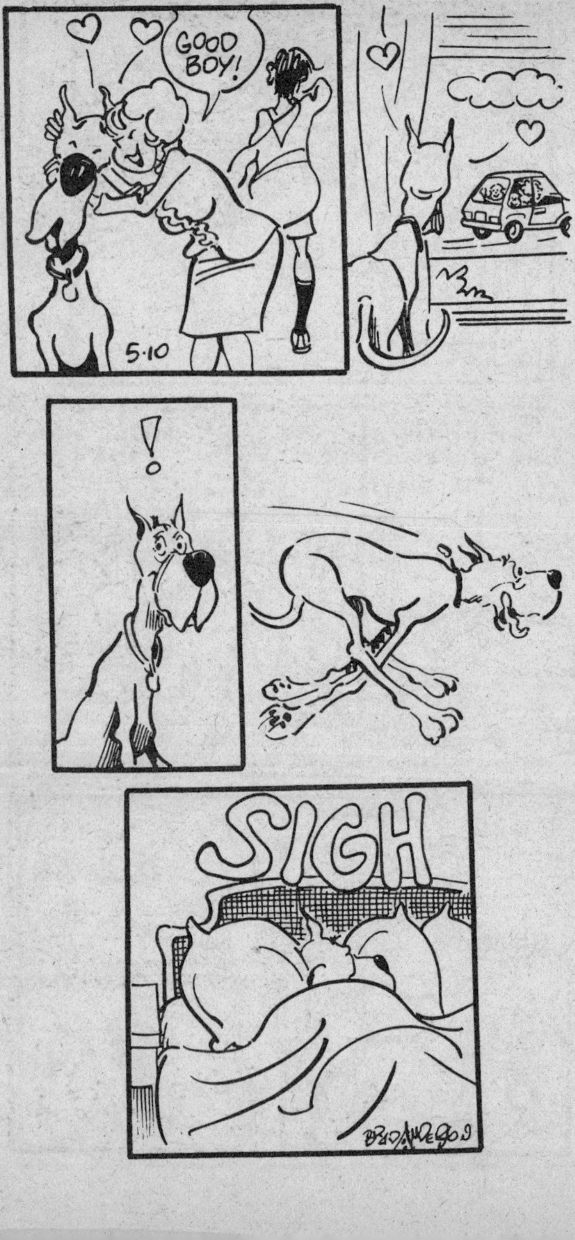
GOOD BOY!
5·10
!
SIGH

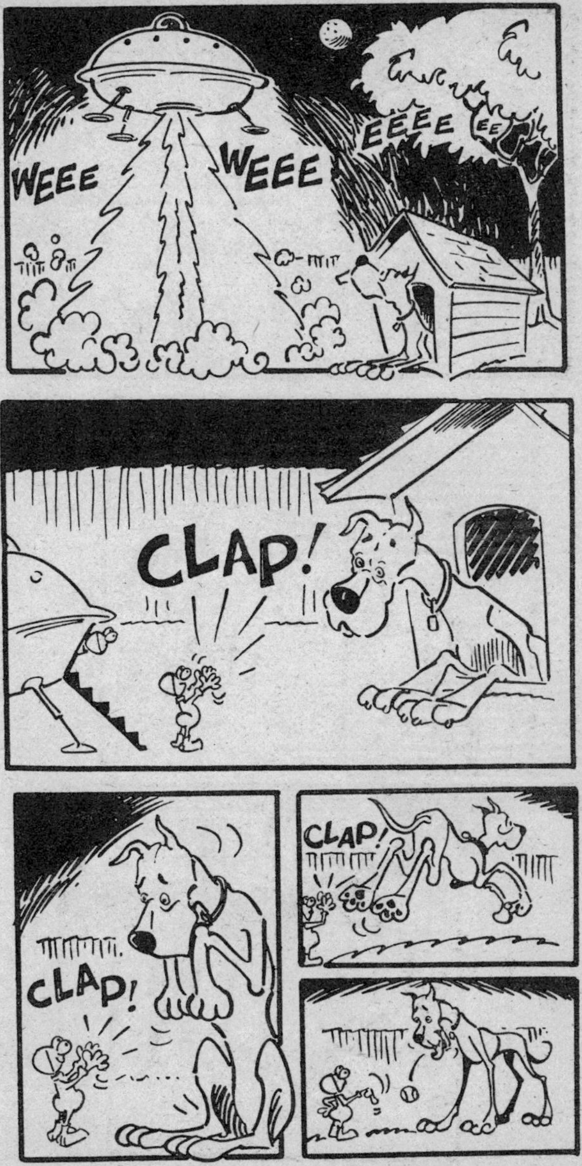
WEEE
WEEE
EEEEE
CLAP!
CLAP!
CLAP!

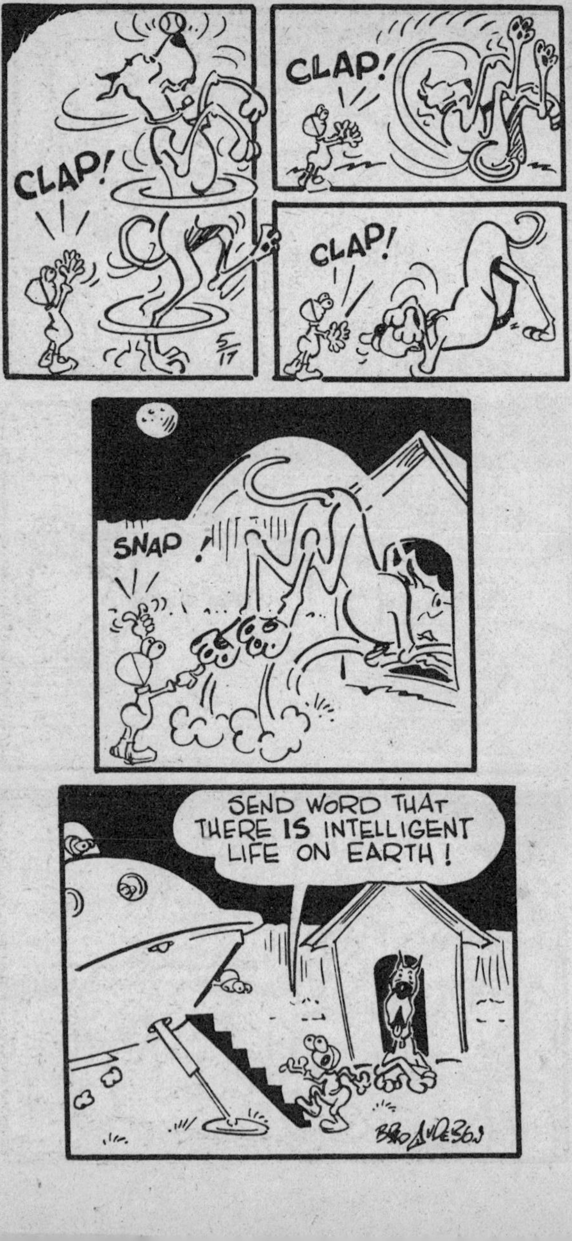
CLAP!
5/17
CLAP!
CLAP!
SNAP!
SEND WORD THAT THERE **IS** INTELLIGENT LIFE ON EARTH!

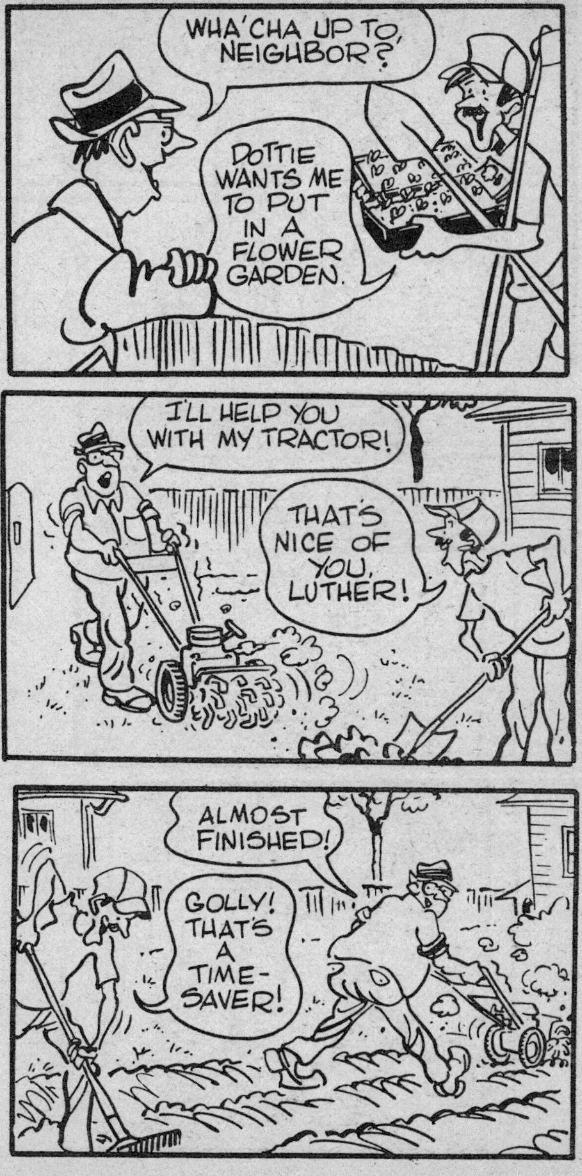
WHA'CHA UP TO, NEIGHBOR?
DOTTIE WANTS ME TO PUT IN A FLOWER GARDEN.
I'LL HELP YOU WITH MY TRACTOR!
THAT'S NICE OF YOU, LUTHER!
ALMOST FINISHED!
GOLLY! THAT'S A TIME-SAVER!

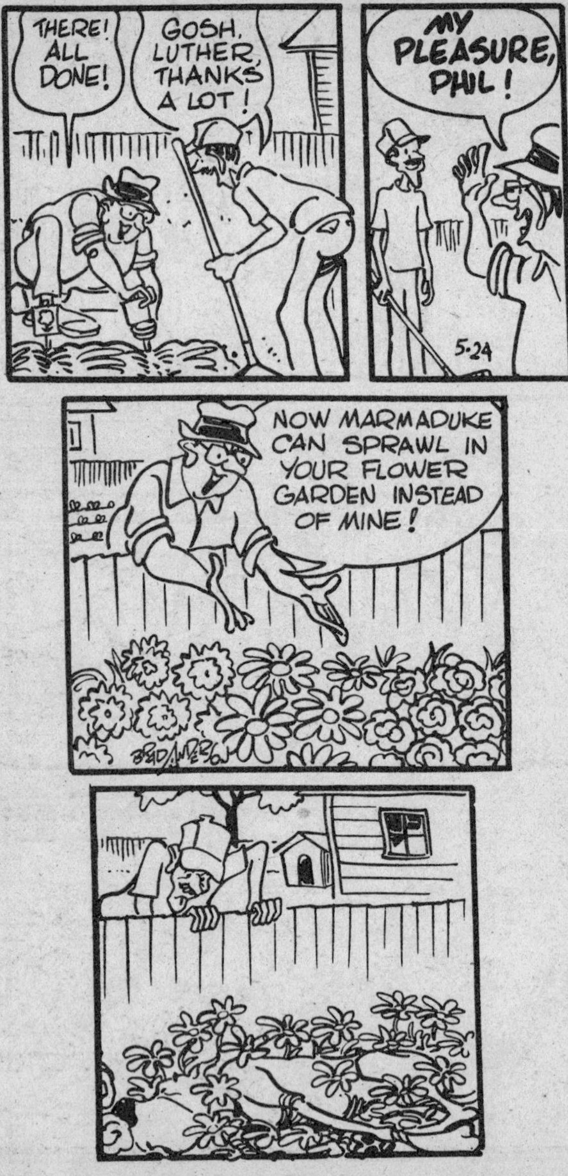
THERE! ALL DONE!
GOSH, LUTHER, THANKS A LOT!
MY PLEASURE, PHIL!
5-24
NOW MARMADUKE CAN SPRAWL IN YOUR FLOWER GARDEN INSTEAD OF MINE!

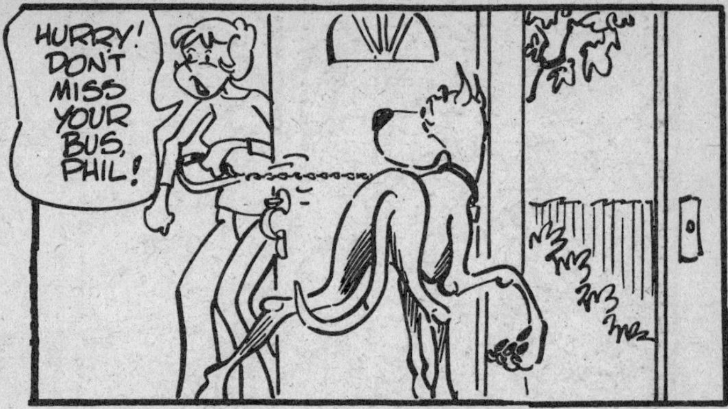
HURRY! DON'T MISS YOUR BUS, PHIL!

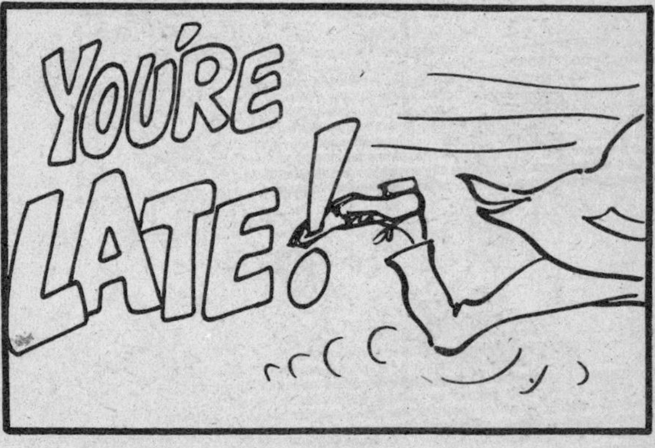
YOU'RE LATE!

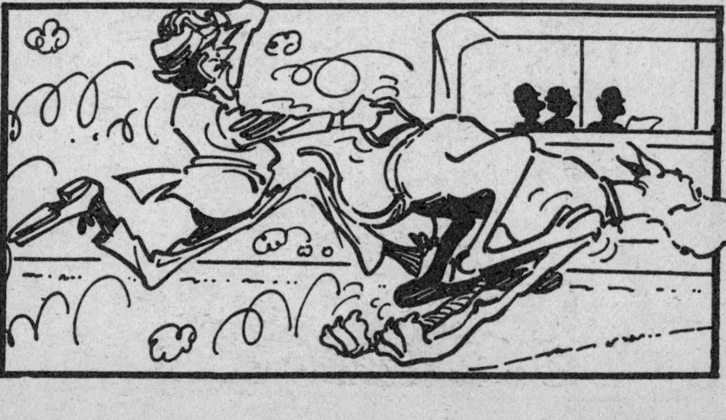

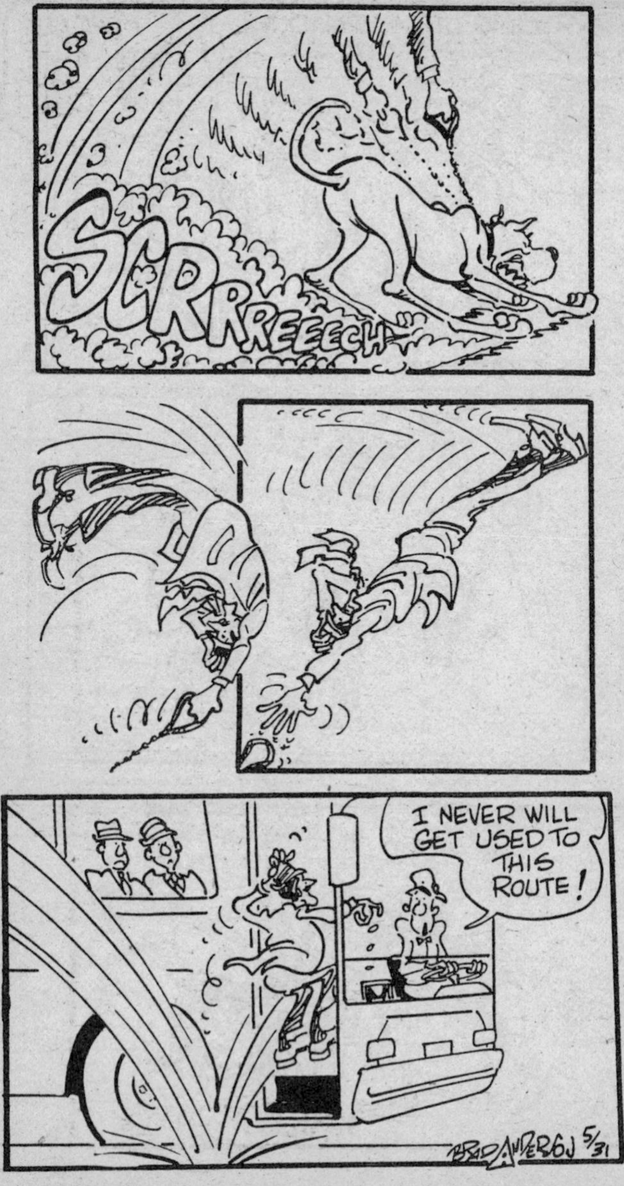
SCRRREEECH
I NEVER WILL GET USED TO THIS ROUTE!
BRAD ANDERSON 5/31

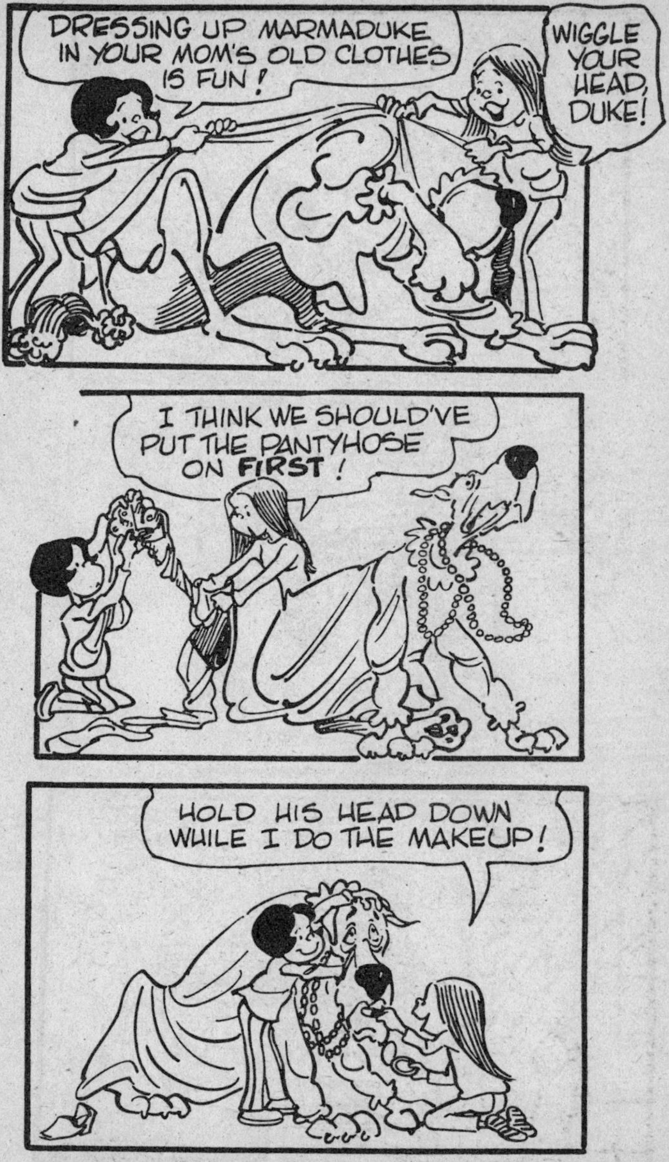
DRESSING UP MARMADUKE IN YOUR MOM'S OLD CLOTHES IS FUN!
WIGGLE YOUR HEAD, DUKE!
I THINK WE SHOULD'VE PUT THE PANTYHOSE ON FIRST!
HOLD HIS HEAD DOWN WHILE I DO THE MAKEUP!

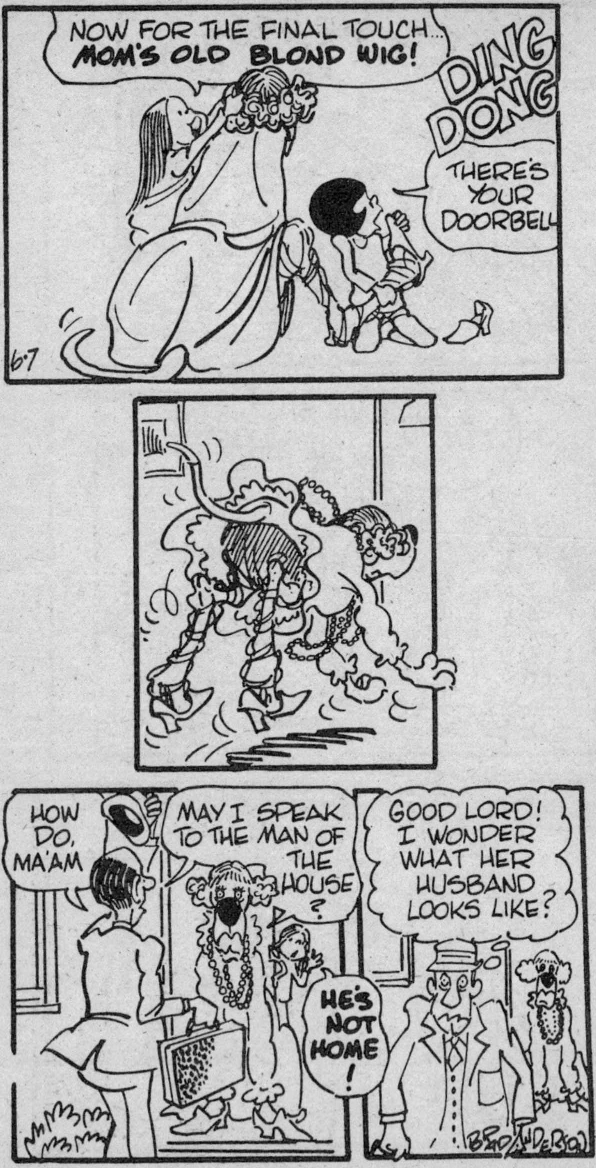
NOW FOR THE FINAL TOUCH... **MOM'S OLD BLOND WIG!**
DING DONG
THERE'S YOUR DOORBELL
6·7
HOW DO, MA'AM
MAY I SPEAK TO THE MAN OF THE HOUSE?
HE'S NOT HOME!
GOOD LORD! I WONDER WHAT HER HUSBAND LOOKS LIKE?

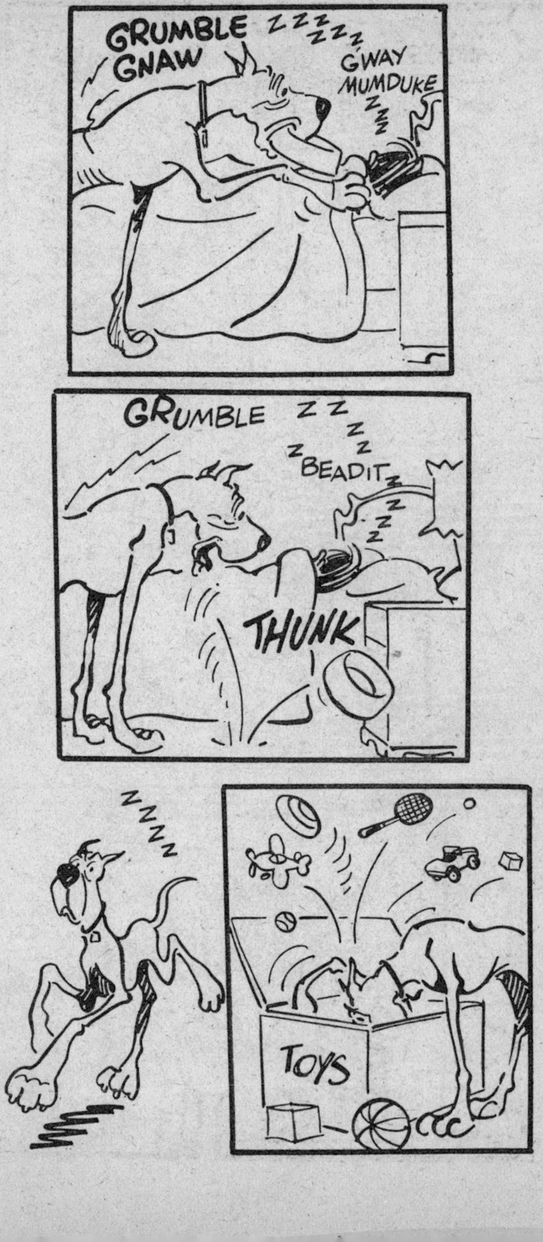
GRUMBLE
GNAW
G'WAY MUMDUKE
GRUMBLE
BEADIT
THUNK
TOYS

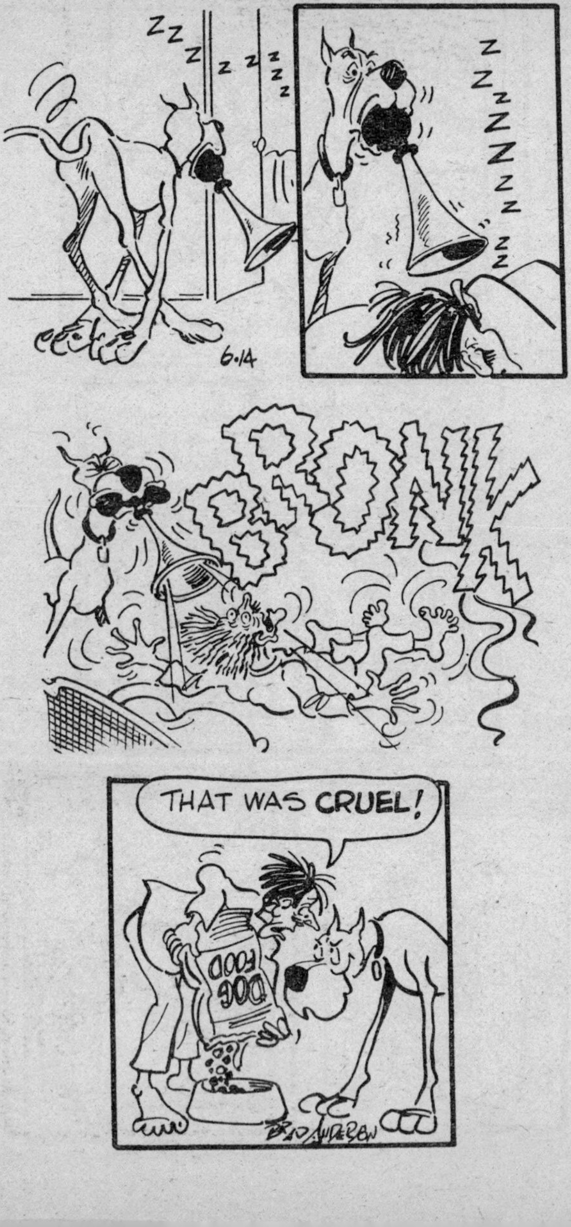
6.14
BONK
THAT WAS CRUEL!
DOG FOOD
BRAD ANDERSON

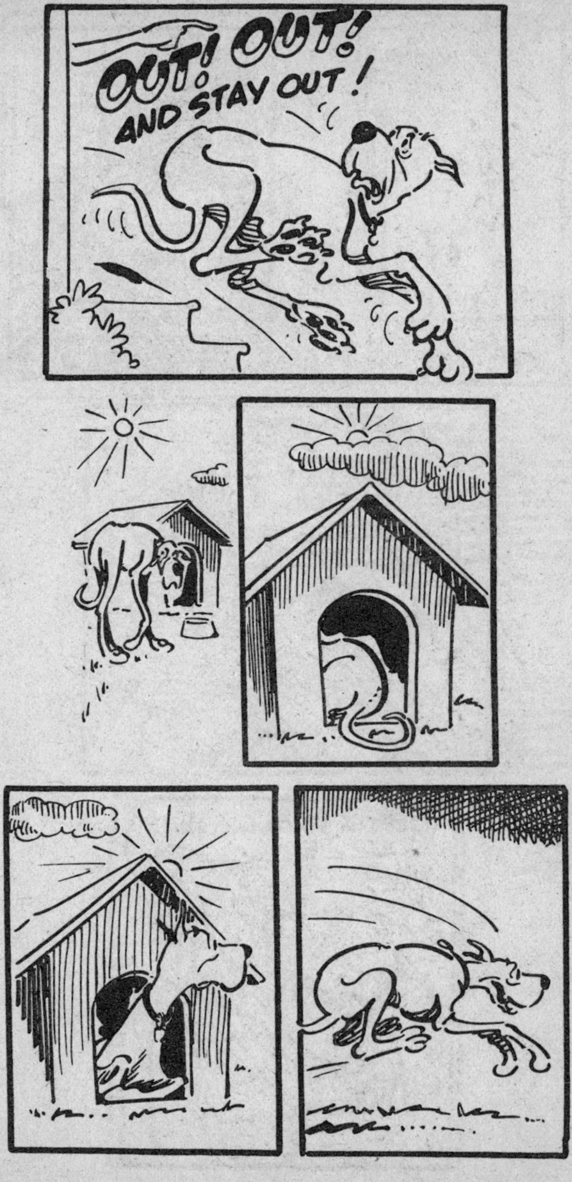
OUT! OUT!
AND STAY OUT!

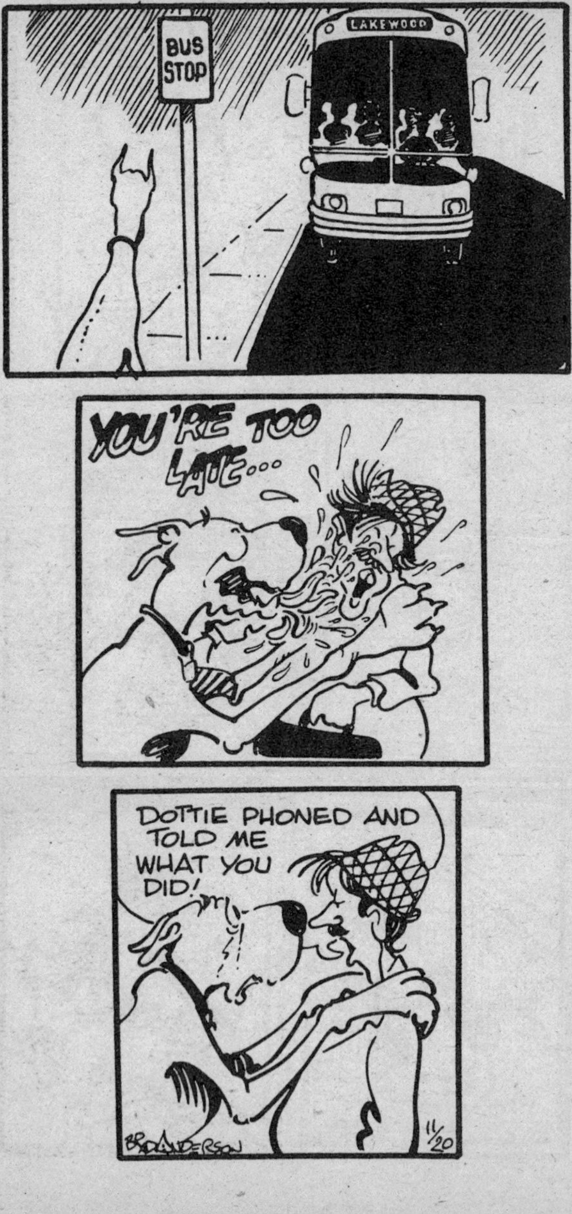
BUS STOP
LAKEWOOD
YOU'RE TOO LATE...
DOTTIE PHONED AND TOLD ME WHAT YOU DID!
BRAD ANDERSON
11/20

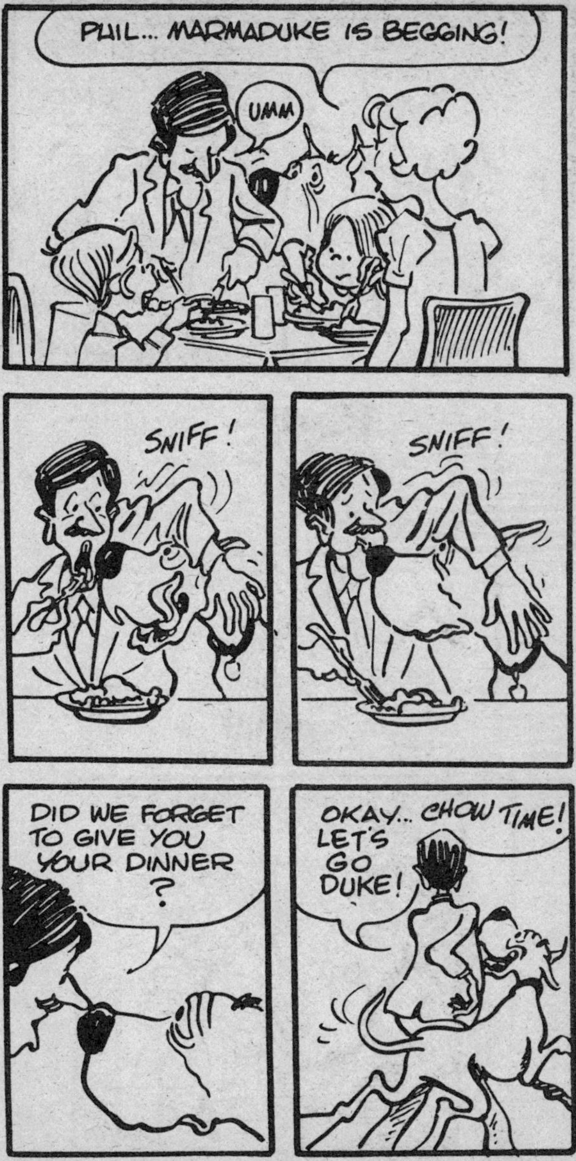
PHIL... MARMADUKE IS BEGGING!
UMM
SNIFF!
SNIFF!
DID WE FORGET TO GIVE YOU YOUR DINNER ?
OKAY... CHOW TIME! LET'S GO DUKE!

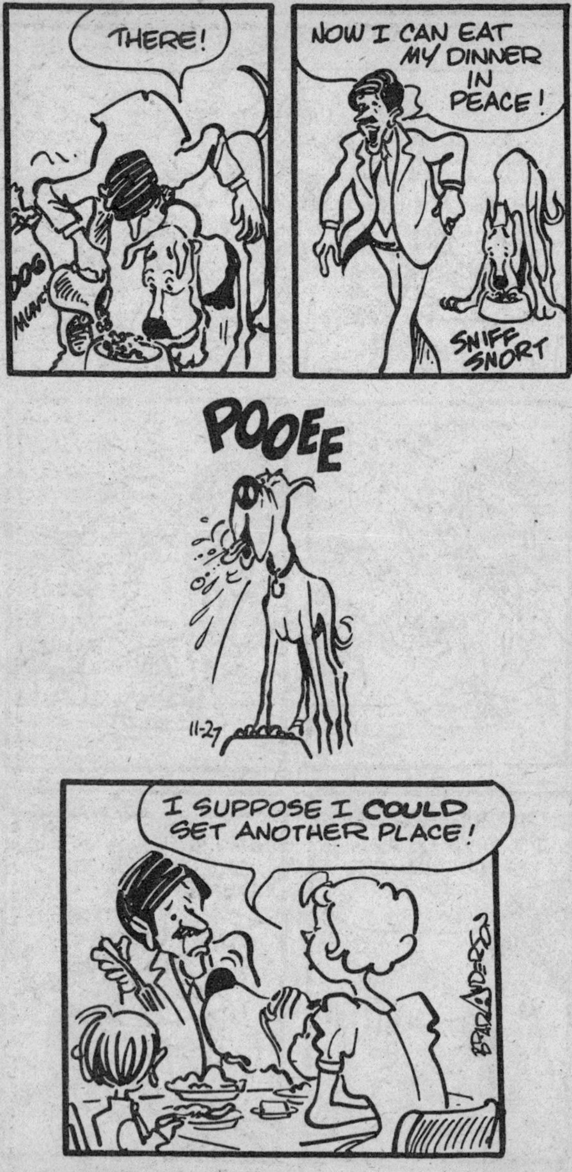
THERE!
NOW I CAN EAT MY DINNER IN PEACE!
SNIFF SNORT
POOEE
11-27
I SUPPOSE I COULD SET ANOTHER PLACE!
BRAD ANDERSON

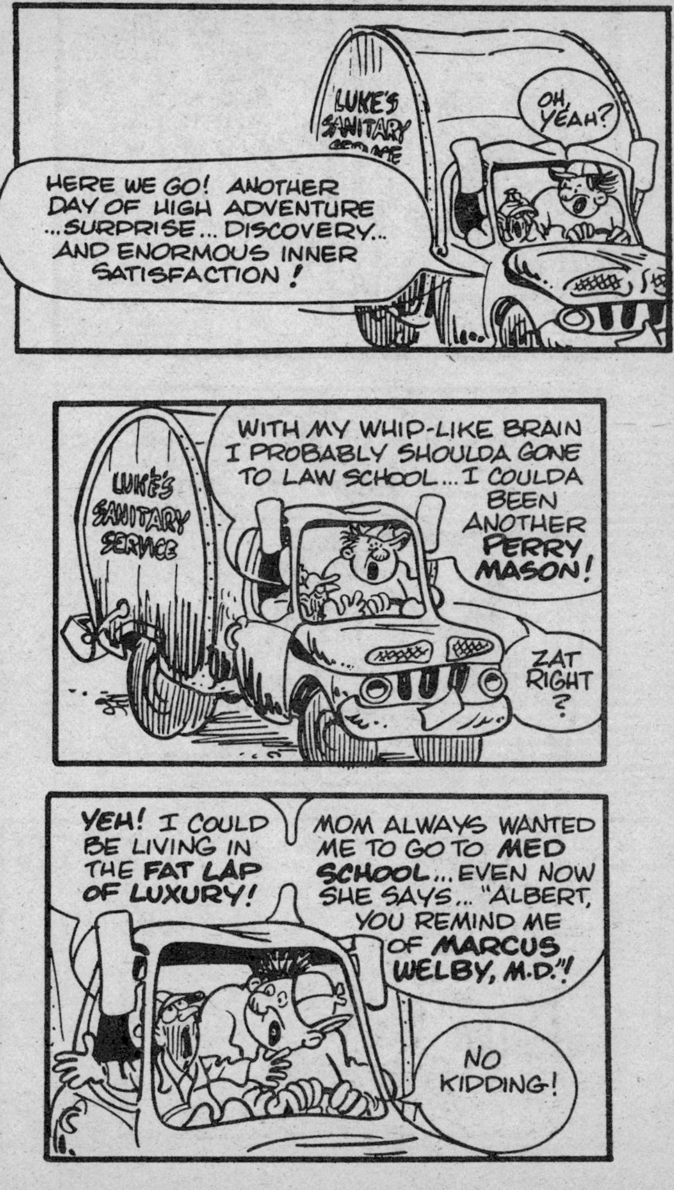
LUKE'S SANITARY SERVICE
OH, YEAH?
HERE WE GO! ANOTHER DAY OF HIGH ADVENTURE ...SURPRISE... DISCOVERY... AND ENORMOUS INNER SATISFACTION!
LUKE'S SANITARY SERVICE
WITH MY WHIP-LIKE BRAIN I PROBABLY SHOULDA GONE TO LAW SCHOOL... I COULDA BEEN ANOTHER PERRY MASON!
ZAT RIGHT?
YEH! I COULD BE LIVING IN THE FAT LAP OF LUXURY!
MOM ALWAYS WANTED ME TO GO TO MED SCHOOL... EVEN NOW SHE SAYS... "ALBERT, YOU REMIND ME OF MARCUS WELBY, M.D."!
NO KIDDING!

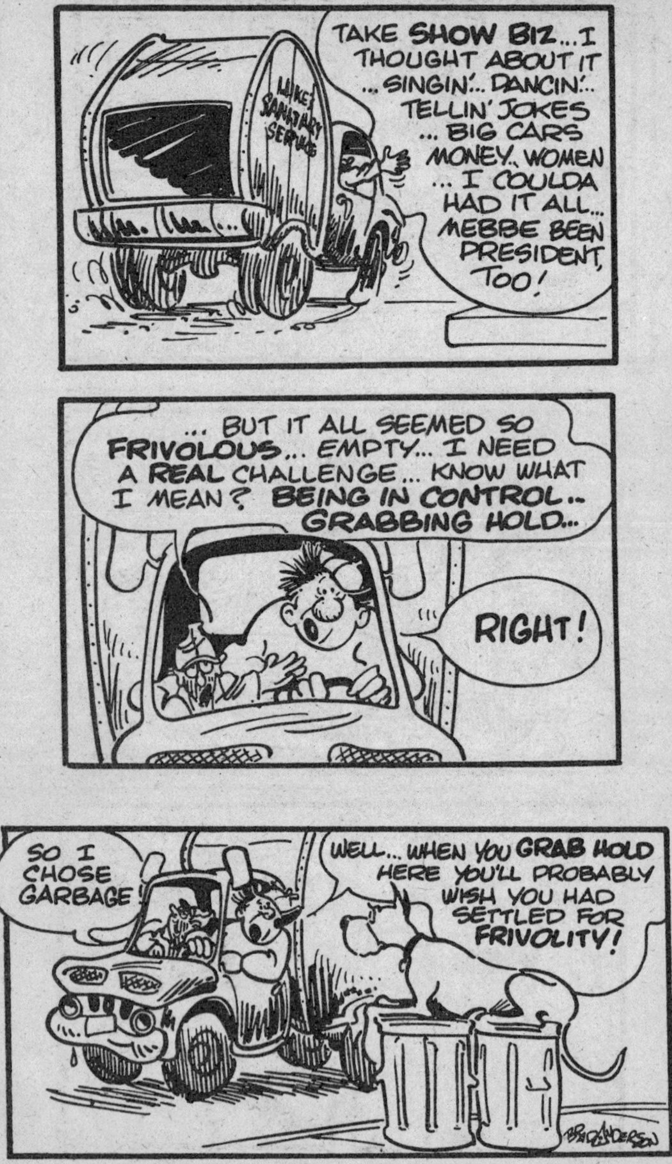
TAKE SHOW BIZ... I THOUGHT ABOUT IT ... SINGIN'... DANCIN'... TELLIN' JOKES ... BIG CARS ... MONEY... WOMEN ... I COULDA HAD IT ALL... MEBBE BEEN PRESIDENT, TOO!
... BUT IT ALL SEEMED SO FRIVOLOUS... EMPTY... I NEED A REAL CHALLENGE... KNOW WHAT I MEAN? BEING IN CONTROL.. GRABBING HOLD...
RIGHT!
SO I CHOSE GARBAGE!
WELL... WHEN YOU GRAB HOLD HERE YOU'LL PROBABLY WISH YOU HAD SETTLED FOR FRIVOLITY!
BRAD ANDERSON

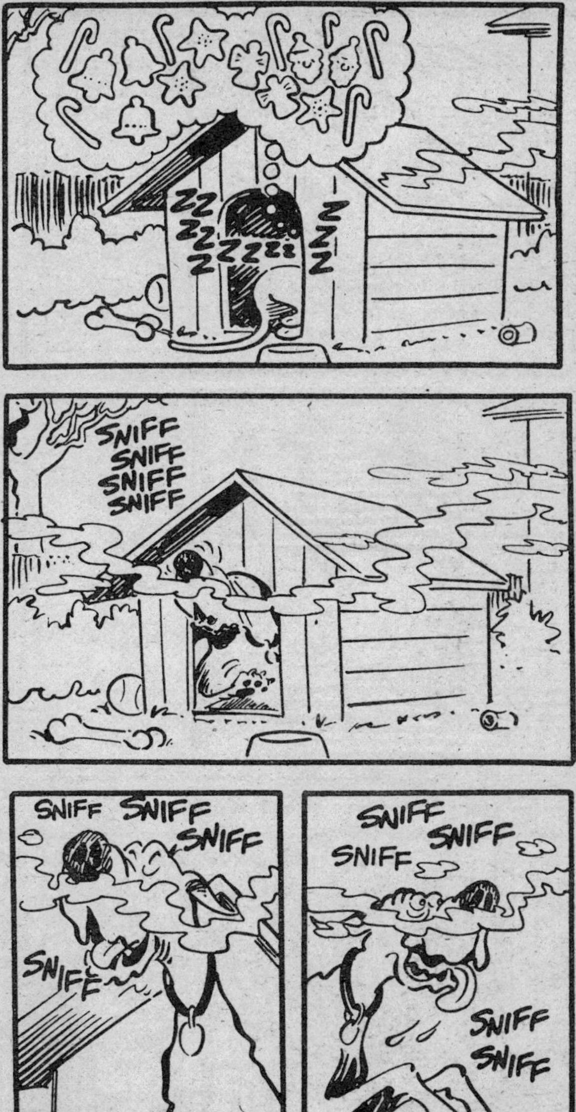

SNIFF
SNIFF
SNIFF
SNIFF
SNIFF SNIFF
SNIFF
SNIFF
SNIFF
SNIFF
SNIFF
SNIFF
SNIFF

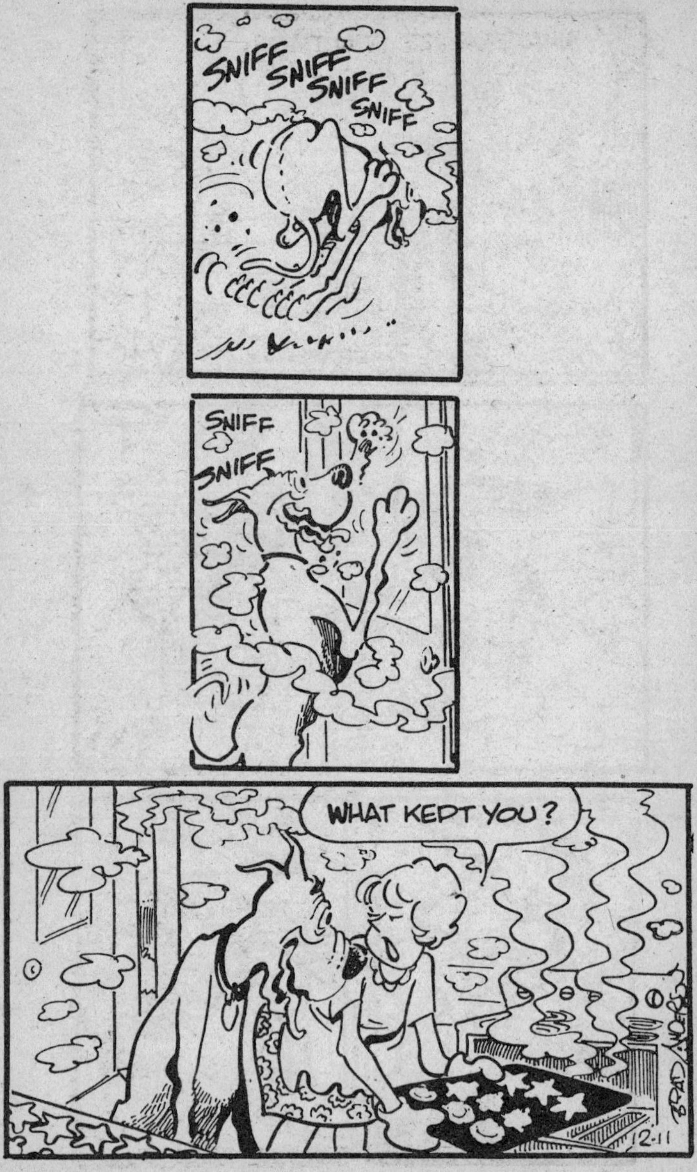
SNIFF SNIFF SNIFF SNIFF
SNIFF SNIFF
WHAT KEPT YOU?
BRAD ANDERSON
12-11

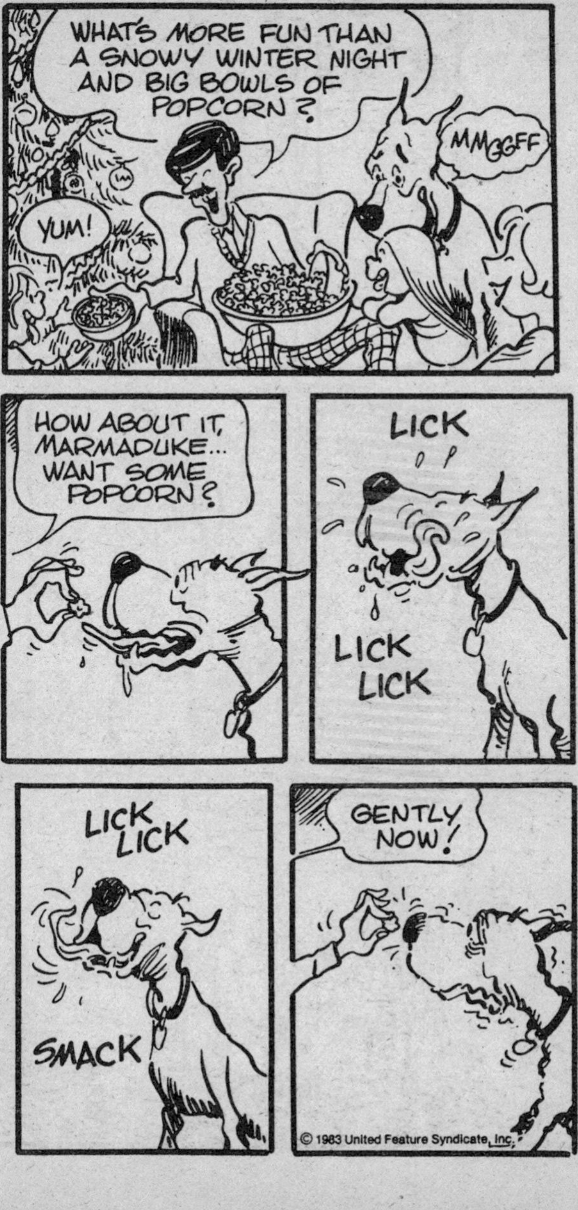

WHAT'S MORE FUN THAN A SNOWY WINTER NIGHT AND BIG BOWLS OF POPCORN?
YUM!
MMGGFF
HOW ABOUT IT, MARMADUKE... WANT SOME POPCORN?
LICK
LICK LICK
LICK LICK
SMACK
GENTLY NOW!
© 1983 United Feature Syndicate, Inc.

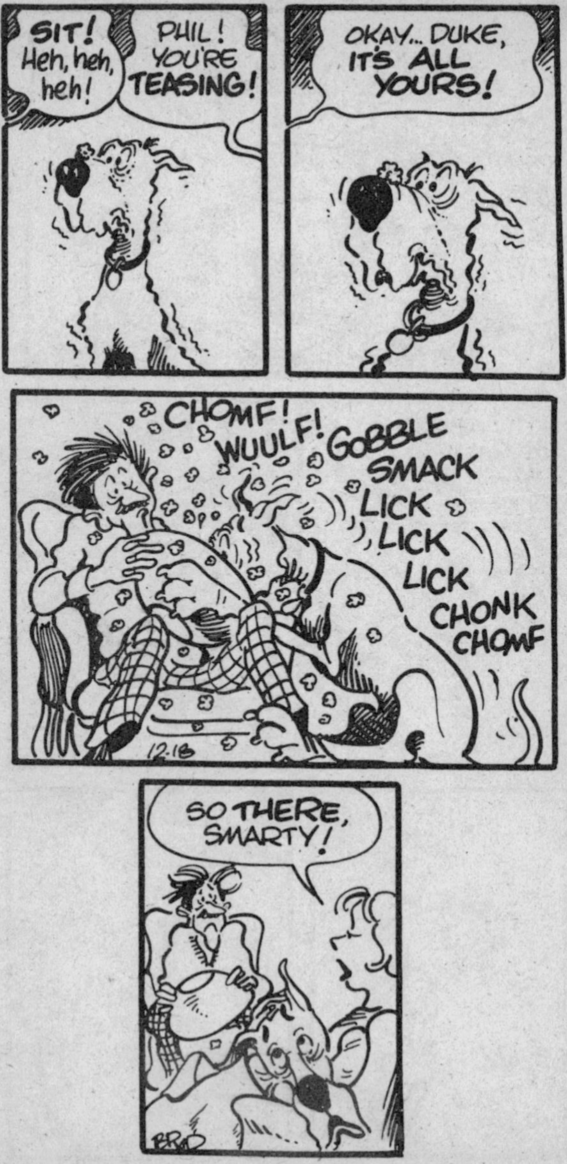
SIT! Heh, heh, heh!
PHIL! YOU'RE TEASING!
OKAY... DUKE, IT'S ALL YOURS!
CHOMF!
WUULF!
GOBBLE
SMACK
LICK
LICK
LICK
CHONK
CHOMF
12.18
SO THERE, SMARTY!
BRAD